To Every You
I've Loved Before

Seven Seas press and purchase enquiries can be sent to
Marketing Manager Lianne Sentar at press@gomanga.com.
Information regarding the distribution and purchase of
digital editions is available from Digital Manager CK Russell
at digital@gomanga.com.

Seven Seas and the Seven Seas logo are trademarks of
Seven Seas Entertainment. All rights reserved.

Follow Seven Seas Entertainment online at
sevenseasentertainment.com.

TRANSLATION: Molly Lee
COVER DESIGN: H. Qi
INTERIOR LAYOUT & DESIGN: Clay Gardner
COPY EDITOR: Catherine Langford
PROOFREADER: Dayna Abel
LIGHT NOVEL EDITOR: T. Burke
PREPRESS TECHNICIAN: Melanie Ujimori, Jules Valera
PRODUCTION MANAGER: Lissa Pattillo
EDITOR-IN-CHIEF: Julie Davis
ASSOCIATE PUBLISHER: Adam Arnold
PUBLISHER: Jason DeAngelis

ISBN: 978-1-68579-727-0
Printed in Canada
First Printing: June 2023
10 9 8 7 6 5 4 3 2 1

To Every You
I've Loved Before

written by
Yomoji Otono

translation by
Molly Lee

Seven Seas

Seven Seas Entertainment

Table of *Contents*

To Every You
I've Loved Before

Prologue...
or Epilogue

WHEN CANCER PATIENTS approach the end of their life, they may choose to decline treatment or hospice care to instead spend their final days in the comfort of their own home. And when my son and his wife suggested I do the same, I felt truly blessed. I didn't want to be a burden on their family, but I trusted that they sincerely wanted to be there for me when my time came. It meant the world to me. And so, I agreed to stay at home under two conditions: no drugs, and no treatments.

At the age of seventy-three, I was perhaps still a bit too young to die, but oddly enough, I felt no fear or regret. I would finish out my life in a large house with my dear wife, my dependable son, my kindhearted daughter-in-law, and my adorable granddaughter. With my family at my side to see me off, even the most excruciating heart failure would be worth it to me. I had lived a good life.

That being said, I needed to make it through the next three days.

"August seventeenth," I said into the wearable device on my left wrist. It displayed an event registered in my calendar.

10 a.m., Showa-dori intersection, Leotard Girl

The Showa-dori intersection was the biggest one our town offered, just a twenty-minute walk from our house. The Leotard Girl was the name of the statue that stood there.

But...I couldn't for the life of me remember making those plans.

At the end of each month, my device would list out the following month's scheduled events. That was how I learned of this one—but who was I meant to meet up with? When did I even add this event? I simply couldn't recall.

Well...could someone else have put it in for me? These devices were operated via voice recognition, so theoretically it should have been impossible, but there were ways to get around such things. I tried asking my family, but none of them knew about it. My granddaughter even had the audacity to suggest I was having a senior moment!

Obviously, I didn't want to believe I could possibly be *that* senile...but on the other hand, I couldn't think of a reason for my family to lie to me about it. Lately, I was starting to think perhaps I really *was* going batty. But regardless of who made the calendar event, I could discover the truth by going to the Showa-dori intersection three days from now at 10 a.m., and I was sorely looking forward to finding out. That was the reason I simply could not afford to kick the bucket in the next three days.

I switched off my bedside lamp and settled into bed. Once I woke up tomorrow morning, there would be just two days left to go. Fortunately, my condition was better than usual as of late, so I was optimistic that I would have no trouble going on a twenty-minute walk. I hadn't visited the intersection in quite a while, and my heart raced like a young boy's at the thought.

But just as I was closing my eyes and hoping to have a pleasant dream, I heard a knock at my door and lifted my lids once more.

"Come in! Door's unlocked," I called, still flat on my back. I reached out to turn my lamp back on. My visitor shyly peeked her head in—it was my ten-year-old granddaughter, Ai.

"Sorry, Grandpa, were you sleeping?"

"No, no. I only just climbed into bed."

"How are you feeling?" she asked.

"Not too bad."

"Can we talk?"

"Of course, sweetheart! Come on in."

She stepped inside, quietly shutting the door behind her, but whatever she came here to say, she seemed hesitant to come right out with it. This was highly unusual for her, as most days, "meek" was just about the last word I'd use to describe her. What was holding her back this time?

"What's the matter? Don't be shy now," I prompted her in my kindest tone of voice. I sat up in bed.

Even when it comes to family, humans tend to be strict on the same sex and soft on the opposite. As such, Ai seemed to prefer her kindly old grandpa over her naggy grandma. But of course,

Grandma loved Ai just as much as I did, and it was thanks to her discipline that I was free to spoil the girl rotten.

Hanging her head, Ai walked to my bedside. She then buried her face in my chest and began to cry.

Now that I thought about it, she usually came to see me first thing after she got home from school, but today had been different. Did something upsetting happen at school? Instead of asking, however, I simply stroked her hair in silence. Eventually, after getting her tears out for a while, she began to tell her story through sniffles.

From what I could piece together, it was really nothing major. Put simply, she had told a boy in her class that she liked him, but he didn't return her feelings. Of course, while part of me felt that ten was a little early to have crushes on boys, I wasn't about to belittle her pain. Nevertheless, I couldn't help but feel relief that the cause was merely rejection.

"I... I never should have told him...!" she cried.

But while I found her circumstances relatively trivial, to *her*, it was practically the end of the world. Hoping to ease that pain, I gave her a pat on the back. "Here, let Grandpa see your IP."

I took her hand and pointed to the IP band on her wrist. She looked up at me, confusion in her puffy eyes. She then tapped her device. On the holographic screen, below "IEPP" was a six-digit numerical display with three integers and three decimals. The decimals were in constant flux, too rapid to follow with the human eye, but the integers held firm at 000.

As a fifth grader, Ai had surely already learned what this meant.

"You may think you never should have told him, but that's not true at all. You were very brave today, Ai. Grandpa's so proud of you."

"How come...?"

"They've already taught you about parallel worlds in school, haven't they?"

"Yeah..."

"By confessing your feelings, you created new possibilities in other worlds! You may have been rejected in this one, but somewhere out there, he likes you back!"

"So what if some other him likes some other me? *I'm* the one who got rejected! It's worthless!"

"That's not true. Every you is still *you*, Ai. You've shifted two or three worlds away before, haven't you?" I asked.

"A few times, yeah."

"In those other worlds, did you still love your grandpa?"

"Of course!" she replied.

"Thank you. Likewise, Grandpa loves any version of you that visits."

"Right..."

"Parallel worlds are where all our unachieved possibilities take form. Somewhere out there, your bravery paid off. The version of you whose crush is mutual is still the same you. So in other words, your heartfelt confession was absolutely *not* worthless."

"I...don't get it..."

Perhaps it was too much for a fifth grader. Besides, everyone had the right to have their own opinion on parallel worlds. I know that back in my day, I really agonized over mine. But while my sweet granddaughter now pouted in confusion, her tears had at least dried. What a rotten grown-up trick it was to distract her from her pain by making her think about something else.

"Okay then, let's make it simple. By getting rejected, you now have the possibility of loving anyone else in the whole world. Trust me, you will meet an even more wonderful young man one day, and you will fall in love again."

"More wonderful? Like who?"

"Hmmm... Like your grandpa?"

"No! I want somebody my own age!" Ai exclaimed.

Ouch. That actually stung a bit.

Regardless, she seemed to have cheered up. Were children simply more resilient? Or would she cry again once she was alone? As I watched her leave the room, I sank back into bed and switched my lamp off. I closed my eyes to prepare for the next day.

What if Ai woke up tomorrow in a parallel world where her feelings were returned? Would this fleeting happiness confuse her? Perhaps she wouldn't want to come home...or perhaps she would find that her crush wasn't as great as she thought he was.

As for me, I'd talk to the parallel Ai who shifted here. How had my parallel self congratulated her when he found out? I suspected I could already find the words.

• • •

Unfortunately, three days later, I wasn't feeling well at all. But I concealed it from my family and left the house with just my wallet and my pills.

"Be back in a bit!"

"Yes, dear. Be careful."

Considering how long we'd known each other, I sensed that my wife might have seen right through me—but if she did, she didn't pry. This was another perk of a long marriage. And so, on August 17th at 9:30 a.m., I headed off to the Showa-dori intersection.

Walking was too difficult for me now, so I took my trusty old motorized wheelchair. That thing could go up to ten kilometers per hour if I really tried, but I was in no real rush. Instead, I chugged along at a buttery smooth four KPH, gazing out at the streets I once traveled on my own two feet.

For some reason, I was in the mood to wax nostalgic. *That building wasn't there before; what did they do with the sculpture? How hasn't that store shut down by now?* The ghosts of old memories sprang to life behind my eyes like two rolls of film played at once. After all, this was most likely my very last trip into town.

It was in that moment I realized I had dawdled a bit too long. I meant to arrive at the meetup spot ten minutes early, but when I checked the time, it was already nearly 10 a.m.

The Showa-dori intersection was our city's largest, splitting into four quarters almost exactly at the center. Styled as a pedestrian scramble, it naturally got a lot of traffic. In the past, there used to be a big pedestrian overpass connecting each of the four corners, but people complained about the pillars impeding visibility for drivers, so the whole thing was torn down. *The old photographs made it look so cool though!* Whenever I came to the intersection, I'd often stop and imagine what it would have been like to walk across it.

But while this place certainly held some dear memories for me...I still couldn't recall what this appointment was for.

Today, 10 a.m., at the Showa-dori intersection—a mysterious calendar entry I didn't remember adding. I had hoped faintly that my so-called "senior moment" would clear away as soon as I got here, but evidently not.

On the southwest corner of the intersection, there was a patch of greenery too small to be called a park. There stood the Leotard Girl, a bronze statue of a curvy young woman shyly covering her chest with her arms. It had been there since before I was born, and I was used to seeing it, but I had no clue who the model was or why it was erected there.

This was supposedly our meetup spot, but other than the people waiting at the crosswalk, I didn't see anyone standing there. I rolled to a stop and gazed up at the statue for a while. Soon after, I felt people staring at me and I hastily looked away.

The next thing I knew, the light had changed, and the crowd on the street corner was gone. A new crowd was approaching from the other side of the road to take their place. Granted, this sleepy little suburban intersection was nothing compared to the big ones I'd seen on TV, but nevertheless, I found myself watching people come and go. Long after they all made it safely across, the light held firm, affording plenty of extra time for pedestrians.

But just then...I spotted a girl standing all alone on the crosswalk. She was just a few steps from the curb, but she refused to finish crossing, nor did she turn back. Instead, she merely stood there.

Of course, the crossing light wouldn't stay green forever. If she waited any longer, she'd be in danger. Rolling my wheelchair to the curb, I called out to her.

"Hello there, young lady! What are you doing there? It's not safe, you know."

At the sound of my voice, the girl looked over. Was she in junior high, perhaps? She was a pretty young girl with long, straight black hair cascading over her white dress.

The moment she laid eyes on me, she tilted her head. "Oh, did you come to get me?" she asked innocently.

A bit of an exaggeration, perhaps, but in a sense, I was indeed retrieving her from the road. Then the walk light started to flash, so I decided to go along with it. "Yes, I've come to get you! Come over here and let's go."

As I spoke, I extended a hand. In response, the girl beamed brightly...and vanished.

I froze with my hand outstretched.

The light then changed, and cars started whizzing past right in front of me, so I put my wheelchair in reverse and went all the way back to the statue. I looked back at the road from there, but still there was no sign of the girl.

This was not my first time seeing someone vanish right before my eyes, but it had been a while, so it really caught me off guard. There could be only one explanation: I had just parallel shifted to an alternate universe. Put simply, my consciousness had traded places with some other self in some other world.

The fact that I was still in the same location suggested that the other me had also come here, which would suggest this world was nearby. However, people didn't vanish into thin air over a difference of two or three worlds, so I must have shifted about ten away. It had been quite some time since my last long-distance shift. Worst-case scenario, back in World Zero, that girl just got hit by a car.

Then, I remembered I hadn't even bothered to check my IP. For all I knew, I could have woken up this morning in a parallel world and only just now returned. Speaking into my IP band, I pulled up the IEPP screen with its six-digit numerical display. If the first three were zero, that meant I was at home in World Zero.

But instead, the screen displayed one word:

ERROR

"It's broken...?"

Oh dear. How was I supposed to know what world I was in now?

If I was currently in World Zero and that girl at the crosswalk was from some other parallel world, then there was nothing I could do—but if *this* was a parallel world and she was from *my* world, well, I had reason to be concerned. Would my parallel self manage to rescue her in my place?

I felt myself growing desperate for some way to check my current IP. I thought about asking a passerby, but then I remembered one snag—someone else's IP wouldn't help me. Alternatively, I could go and request a replacement, but that process would take hours.

As I mulled it over, it occurred to me that human beings had lived happily for thousands of years with no way of checking their IP at all. But then, a single scientist came along and proved the existence of parallel worlds, revealing that we all unconsciously shifted across them on a daily basis. Now, decades later, elementary school students were learning about it alongside their other subjects—something that was previously seen as nothing more than science fiction.

In essence, I had just gone back to the way life used to be.

I could still remember the day that the concept of parallel worlds came crashing into my life. Yes, the day I became aware of other worlds was right around my tenth birthday...

To Every You
I've Loved Before

CHAPTER 1

Childhood

A T AGE SEVEN, I understood what "divorce" was, and when my parents asked me to choose one of them to live with, I didn't throw a fit.

My father was a celebrated researcher in his field while my mother came from a wealthy family. No matter who I chose, I would have all the financial security I needed, so I was free to let my heart decide—and ultimately, I chose my mother. Not because I loved her more than my father, but because I was afraid I would get in the way of his work if I was around.

The root cause of their divorce was poor communication. My father spent many a night at his laboratory, and whenever he came home, he would tell my mother all about his work. Naturally, to her, it was total gibberish. Alas, my father was the kind of man who automatically assumed everyone else understood all the same things he did, and I often watched my mother struggle in conversations with him while he remained blissfully unaware.

Therefore, based on their personalities, I decided Mom was the better choice. Well, no—I'm sure my thought process at age seven wasn't quite that clear-cut, but you get the point.

Ironically, the divorce dramatically improved my parents' relationship, and they cheerfully traded me back and forth at least once a month. Obviously, they had to have loved each other very much considering they got married and had a child in the first place, but it was clear this degree of separation was healthy for them. Personally, I was just happy that they stopped fighting and relieved that it wasn't because of me.

What I remember most strongly from my childhood was that just a few months after my mother and I moved in with her parents, my father bought me an airsoft gun.

Mom and I went to the park one sunny weekend to meet up with him. I thought I would really miss him now that I only saw him once a month instead of every day, but his work hours were so irregular that I hadn't really spent that much quality time with him prior to the divorce. If anything, now that we were going on scheduled monthly outings as a family, he was arguably more present in my life than ever.

"Koyomi!"

My father said my name for the first time in a month. How often had he called for me back when we all lived together? I couldn't really remember. But considering I now felt so happy hearing the sound of my own name, perhaps this new relationship wasn't so bad.

"Is there anything on your wish list, kiddo?"

My eighth birthday was just a couple of days prior to that visit, so he probably wanted to get me a belated present. Before the divorce, Mom was the only one who ever bought me stuff, so the prospect of a gift from Dad delighted me. And as it happened, there *was* something I was hoping to get...

"An airsoft gun!"

"An *airsoft gun*? What for?"

"Everybody at school has one except me!"

"Huh. Where do they even sell them...?"

Luckily, I knew the answer to that! One of my classmates bragged to me that his parents had bought one for him in the toy aisle of a certain department store. I dragged Mom and Dad to the store and found the shelf with a few airsoft guns still in stock. I didn't know anything about the different types—I just wanted to have a cool toy like everyone else had. I grabbed one blindly off the shelf and held it out to Dad.

"This one!"

"Oh, it's cheaper than I thought. Not even 2,000 yen. Okay then..."

But just then, he froze. I looked at him. He was squinting down at the box.

"This says it's for ages ten and up."

Uh-oh. I had only just turned eight. But it went without saying that all my bragging classmates were my same age or younger— clearly, a lot of parents were really cool and didn't fret about the small stuff, right? Was my dad that kind of dad? Sure, *Mom* was the fretting type, but this was a gift from *Dad*, so her opinion didn't matter this time! (Or so I thought. Ah, sweet childhood innocence.)

Either way, if he tried to tell me I was too young for an airsoft gun, I was planning to persuade him by pointing out that all my classmates had one, and that being eight was really no different from being ten, *and* I'd promise to always be careful not to hurt anyone! I had so much prepared to say...but in the end, I was worried for nothing.

"Eh, eight's not that different from ten."

Internally, I did a fist pump. My dad was a cool dad! Unsurprisingly, my mom frowned at this, but she didn't protest—looking back, they'd only just gotten divorced, so she must've been feeling a little guilty towards me at the time. And with that, I got my mitts on an airsoft gun meant for older kids.

Back at the park, I played with my new toy for a bit. After a while, I started feeling hungry, so we had lunch. We all agreed to meet up again a month, and then we parted ways with Dad and headed home.

Back at the house, our big golden retriever jumped up to greet me, tail wagging behind her.

"We're home, Yuno!" I gave her a scritch behind the ears, her favorite.

My grandpa first adopted Yuno right after I was born, and before the divorce, I'd play with her whenever we visited. Now that we lived together, I got to play with her every day! That was definitely one highlight of living here with my grandparents.

"My dad bought me this! Isn't it cool?" I bragged as I showed her the airsoft gun. The dog cocked her head at it. If I pointed it at her, could she learn to play dead like I'd seen some other dogs do on TV?

"Don't you dare point it at Yuno," Mom scolded me lightly, as if she read my mind.

"Okaaay..."

On the way home, she warned me a thousand times not to point it at people. *I get it already! Jeez!* Then, after giving Yuno lots of pets, I went into the living room to say hi to my grandpa.

"We're home, Grandpa!"

"Oh, welcome home, Koyomi. Did you have fun?" he asked with a warm smile. He was a man of few words, but overall he was a nice guy who always gave me candy.

"Sure did! Can I have a piece of candy?"

"You had one earlier! One per day, remember?"

That said, I *did* think he was stingy for refusing to give me more than one per day. He always had my favorite candy, but he kept it squirreled away in a tall drawer that he knew I couldn't reach on my own, all because "too much candy is bad for you."

Ah, but if only I thought a little harder about his personality before I showed him the airsoft gun.

"Fine, whatever. Anyway, check this out!"

"Oh, an airsoft gun! Little boys just love those things, don't they? Why, when I was your age..." A moment later, the serene smile vanished from his face and his eyes hardened. "Let me see that, Koyomi."

"Huh? Okay..." He sounded uncommonly grave, so I obediently handed over the box with the gun inside.

"This says 'ages ten and up.' You're too young," he said firmly, pointing at the label. He then rose to his feet and left the room. When he came back, the airsoft gun was nowhere to be found.

He...threw it away?

I sobbed and wailed, and from that day forward, I hated my grandpa, and I was convinced that he must've hated me too. The more Grandma consoled me, the more attached I grew to her, and soon I stopped talking to Grandpa much at all.

I didn't understand how much he actually loved me until two years later when he passed away...leaving behind a mystery for me to solve.

• • •

"Koyomi!"

I could hear Grandpa calling for me through the sliding paper door. Two years after the airsoft gun incident, I still hated his guts. I didn't even ask him for candy anymore. I was tempted to ignore him and go play outside instead, but he must have heard me stop short. He already knew that I heard him, and I'd get in trouble if I ignored him on purpose. Resigned to my fate, I slid his bedroom door open.

"What is it, Grandpa?"

I walked in with a perfect poker face and found him lying in bed. When we first moved here, he used to sleep on a futon on the floor. After a few hospital stays, he switched to one of those fancy remote-controlled beds instead.

"Come here, please," he said weakly.

His voice was no longer as commanding as it used to be. Mom told me he was sick. *Hurry up and die already,* I thought to myself as I walked to his bedside.

"Want a piece of candy?"

"...No thanks." I hadn't eaten that candy in two years, but I could still remember how sweet it tasted. Deep down, I *did* want it. But for some reason, I couldn't admit it.

"I see," Grandpa muttered, though I couldn't gauge his reaction. He didn't press me further, however. Instead, he grabbed a box off the bedside table and held it out to me. "Koyomi, I wanted to give you this."

"What's in the box?"

It was about the size of a standard spiral notebook, barely weighed anything, and didn't make any sound when I shook it. Maybe it was empty. But the outside looked like a treasure chest, so I was curious. When I tried to open it, however, it refused to budge.

"Grandpa, it won't open."

"Yes, I'm afraid the box is locked."

"Where's the key?" I asked.

"Hidden in a place only I know about," he said.

"Why would you hide it? Just give it to me."

"Don't worry, I'll give you the key before I die."

At that, my heart skipped a beat. Ever since he threw away my airsoft gun, I'd wished for him to die... Had he read my mind somehow?!

"Also..."

He started to say something else, but I was so frightened that I took the box and ran out of the room.

• • •

A few months later, on a weekend, I was getting ready to go hang out with my friends from school after I ate lunch.

"Where are you going, Koyomi?" my mother asked.

I was putting my shoes on at the front door. It was weird she was asking me—I was pretty sure I already told her about it last night. "To hang out with my friends."

"Grandpa's not doing well, sweetie... Mommy needs you to stay home today," she told me in a firm voice. However...

"Yeah, well, I don't care about how Grandpa's doing. Later." And with that, I opened the front door.

"Then at least try to come home early!" she shouted after me, but I ignored her and took off running. Even Yuno barked at me as I left, something she normally never did.

Regardless, I went off to play with my friends, then came home in the evening like usual. For the record, I made sure to arrive before sundown...but by then, it was too late.

"I'm hooome..."

"Where *were* you, Koyomi?! Mommy told you to come home early!" I could tell from the look on her face that Mom was absolutely furious with me.

"I... I'm sorry... But how come?"

No, she wasn't just furious—she was *crying*. "Grandpa... He...!"

I understood what death meant, as much as any other ten-year-old, anyway. But I didn't have a clue how I was supposed to feel or what I was supposed to say.

"He kept asking for you, over and over... He wanted to see you...!" she yelled.

Her anger quickly gave way to grief, and she started crying again. Grandma was crying too. But...*I* didn't have any tears for Grandpa. He didn't like me, so why would he want to see me? There was one thing on my mind, however.

"Hey, Mom?"

"...Yes?"

"Um... Did Grandpa say anything about, like...a message for me? Or a gift?"

"He was going to give you something?"

"Yeah, he said he'd give me a key."

"What key?" she asked.

I hadn't told anyone about the box he gave me. Even if I didn't like the guy, it was thrilling to have a secret to keep. But as I debated whether to tell her...

"Your grandpa got very sick very suddenly, so maybe he was asking for you because he wanted to give you the key. But...then he...!" She started sobbing again.

Personally, I was more disappointed about the prospect of never being able to open the box than I was about Grandpa dying. If I had known, I would've stayed home to get the key instead of playing with my friends. Where the heck did he put it, anyway? And what was inside the box? Would I ever find out?

Now I was filled with regret. Would I truly never get my hands on that key? Couldn't he come back as a ghost or something real quick? I just really, really, *really* needed to see him one last time—

• • •

But the next thing I knew, I was inside some kind of strange pod.

"...Huh?"

I was lying on a bed of sorts, and in front of me, I could faintly see my reflection in the glass door. I tried pushing it, but it wouldn't budge! *Am I trapped?* I could feel panic creeping in. What the heck was going on?!

One minute I was at home, and my grandpa was dead, and Mom and Grandma were crying...and now I was here. Why? Where was here, anyway?!

I was so confused. I felt the urge to scream for help—but just then, I noticed a figure on the other side of the glass door. It was a girl who looked to be about my age, but I didn't recognize her. Without thinking further, I pounded on the glass; she flinched at the sound. *Uh-oh.* I couldn't afford to scare her away!

"Hey, um, can you hear me? I'd like to get out of this thing, but I can't open it from the inside," I explained. I tried my best to sound friendly.

Luckily, she *was* able to hear me. She started tapping all around the pod, struggling to open it. Then, once I was finally freed, the first thing I did was take a look around. I was in a big white room filled with machines and cables connected to the pod. Looking at it, it was shaped sort of like a cockpit from a mecha anime.

And then there was *her*.

We gazed at each other in silence. She was a pretty girl with long, straight black hair cascading over her white dress. However, I didn't recognize her in the slightest. Still, she had to know something about this place, so I decided to be brave and ask her.

"Um... What's your name? I don't know where I am, or what I'm doing here... Is my mommy here?"

The instant I spoke, the girl turned on her heel and bolted out of the room.

"Hey, wait!" Reflexively, I gave chase.

She weaved her way effortlessly through the cluttered halls, suggesting she knew the place well. I lagged behind farther and farther, and eventually she ran outside through what appeared to be an employee exit. I dashed through it myself a few seconds later. But by the time I made it into the narrow alley, there was no sign of her.

In the dim light of sunset, this building didn't look familiar in the slightest. Perplexed, I walked around to the other side, looking for the main road. There, at what I suspected was the main entrance of the building, I saw a sign that read *IMAGINARY SCIENCE RESEARCH INSTITUTE*. I didn't know what "imaginary science" was supposed to mean, but the rest sounded like the sort of place where my dad worked.

Fortunately, the address was listed right there on the sign. I recognized the street as one that would take about an hour to walk to from my house. *How the heck did I get here? And where are my parents? Or Grandma?* Fear and loneliness overwhelmed me until I was on the verge of tears.

Just then, I saw a kindly-looking woman walking down the street in my direction. When I ran up to her, she stopped short in alarm.

"Sorry to bother you! Can you tell me where I am?" I asked.

"What?"

"What part of Japan is this? City and street?"

"This is Oita City, capital of Oita Prefecture, and we're on XYZ Street," she said.

In that case, it was indeed the same street I thought it was. That much was a relief. Worst-case scenario, I could walk home from here...with a little help, at least.

"Um, do you know where ABC Street is?" I asked.

"Yes, I do."

"Can you tell me how to get there from here?"

"On foot? That'll take you an hour! Can't you ask your mom or dad to pick you up?"

"I don't have a cell phone."

"Then you can borrow mine! Here you are."

And with that, the lady lent me her phone. I was grateful to have bumped into someone as nice as she was. As luck would have it, I had the number to my grandparents' house memorized, so I decided to take her up on it.

"Takasaki residence."

"Mommy?" I asked.

"Koyomi, is that you? What's the matter?" This was not the reaction I'd expected, though she did sound mildly surprised. "Did Daddy buy you a cell phone?"

"No, no! This nice lady is letting me borrow hers," I said.

"What?"

"Look, I don't know how to explain it, but...can you just come get me?"

"Of course, sweetie! But...what about Daddy?"

"Uhhh... I dunno. He's not here."

"I see. I take it you two had a fight or something?"

"Huh?" For some reason, this conversation felt ever so slightly off to me.

"It's not important. Now, where am I picking you up?" Mommy asked.

"I'm at the Imaginary Science Research Institute on XYZ Street."

"So you *are* with Daddy! I'll be right there. We can talk about it in the car."

"Uhhh... Okay...?"

Confused, I hung up and gave the phone back to the kind lady. Then I stood outside the research institute and waited for my mom to come and get me.

Why did she keep asking me about Dad? I hadn't seen him all day. And why didn't she sound sad anymore? Didn't I literally vanish in front of her? No, surely that had to be impossible. Otherwise, she would have been *way* more worried about me.

In that case...could I have walked all the way here with her full permission and I just...couldn't remember doing it? That didn't seem possible either, but surely it was a lot more realistic than teleportation...

As I mulled it over, time flew by, and before I knew it, I heard a car approaching from the end of the sleepy street. It wasn't my mom's car, so I got up and moved away from the curb just in case—but then, inexplicably, the car pulled over right in front of me.

"Huh?"

My mom was in the driver's seat. Weird—normally she drove her brand-new minicar. What was she doing behind the wheel of a crusty old pickup? Upon further inspection, however, I vaguely recognized it from somewhere...

"Oh!"

Now I remembered. This was my grandpa's pickup truck! As far as I knew, it had been gathering dust in the garage over the past few years, but maybe she had decided to start driving it now that Grandpa passed away. I didn't even know there was gas in the tank.

When I hopped into the passenger seat, Mom greeted me with a smile. "Wait, where's Daddy?"

"I told you, he's not here!"

"Huh. Well, what now? Shall I take you home with me?"

I didn't need to go shopping or anything. I just wanted to go home and feel safe again. So that's where I asked her to take me.

"Now tell me, what happened today?" she asked as she drove across town. "Did something bad happen with Daddy?"

Yet again, she brought up my dad. *Why?*

"No, nothing happened. I haven't even seen him today."

"Then what were you doing at the lab?"

"Huh? What does that place have to do with Daddy?"

"Don't be silly! He *works* there, remember?"

This came as a shock. I knew my dad was a scientist at some kind of laboratory, but I didn't know it was that one specifically. "Oh..."

"You actually forgot? Has it been a while since you were last there?"

"What? That was my first visit."

"Wait, really? Daddy told me he's taken you to work with him before."

"Has he...? I'm not sure I remember that..."

"At the very least, this was *not* your first visit. You might not remember, but we took you there a handful of times when you were younger."

Huh. I had absolutely no memory of that, so I must have been really little. But...for some reason I couldn't put my finger on, something about all this felt...*off* somehow. My stomach was twisting into knots.

As we continued this mildly perplexing conversation, we eventually arrived back at home—but I noticed my mom's mini-car was nowhere to be seen. Where was it?

Once I hopped out and walked to the front door, Mom drove the truck around to the garage behind the house. In the meantime, I was hoping to play with Yuno to calm my nerves, but she wasn't outside in the yard. Maybe she was asleep in her doghouse—if so, I wouldn't want to wake her.

Then, the delicious smell of dinnertime instantly reminded me I was hungry, so I walked into the house. "I'm home!"

"Oh? Well, well, well! If it isn't our Koyomi!" Grandma came out from the kitchen to greet me with a smile. *How was she in such a good mood when Grandpa just died?* "I'm so glad to see you. Go on, have a seat! Are you hungry? Dinner will be ready soon."

Had Grandpa's death driven her off the deep end...? After seeing her break down in tears, this "normal" behavior registered as alarming. Nevertheless, I headed to the living room to have a seat, as requested—

And that was when my brain stopped working entirely.

Sitting on the floor at the coffee table...

"Oho, Koyomi, my boy! Long time no see. Come, sit right here next to me."

...my dead grandfather was beckoning to me.

• • •

I could think of a few different theories.

First, this could be a dream. In fact, I hoped it was. But no amount of pinching or slapping my cheeks was helping me wake up.

Second, this Grandpa could be a ghost. After all, I remembered wishing he would come back as one. But when I summoned all my courage to reach out and touch him, he was solid and warm, like a living person.

Third... I really wanted to believe it wasn't the case, but...I could have simply lost my marbles.

With no clue what was going on, my only option was to stay calm and slowly ferret information out of my family. After a short while, I was forced to arrive at a single indisputable conclusion:

This was not my world.

In *this* world, when my parents got divorced three years ago, I had chosen to live with Dad instead of Mom—which would make this a "parallel world," like in an anime or something. In *this* reality, I didn't live in this house; I lived with Dad. That's why Mom kept asking about him, and why Grandma was so excited to see me.

I'm not sure how I accepted this revelation so readily. I wasn't even worried about getting back to my home world. No, there was only one thing on my mind—in this world, Grandpa was still alive, so maybe I could get that key after all!

• • •

It took a lot of courage to talk to Grandpa. After all, back in *my* world, we barely spoke. However, I was dead set on opening that treasure chest, so for the first time in two years, I headed to his bedroom of my own free will.

"Hey, um, Grandpa?"

"That you, Koyomi?" he asked from inside.

"Can we talk for a sec?"

"Of course, of course! Come on in!"

He was so nice to me, it caught me completely off-guard. Back in my world, I was sure he hated my guts, so I was always scared of him. But then I remembered...he *used* to be as nice as this Grandpa, prior to the airsoft gun incident. After that, I avoided him for the next two years, and then he died.

Belatedly, I started to wish I'd talked to him a little more. Maybe we could have patched things up, and he would have given me that key... Now I was even *more* desperate to open the treasure chest. If he was as kind and loving as this world's Grandpa, then what in the world was his parting gift to me?

"Hey Grandpa, do you have a treasure chest?"

"A treasure chest? Can't say I do."

Apparently, this wasn't going to be quite that easy. This version of Grandpa didn't even have the box my world's Grandpa had given to me. Maybe it was something he bought just for me—in that case, it made sense that this Grandpa didn't have one. After all, my parallel self didn't even live here.

"Need a box for something? I've got plenty of old candy tins you can use," Grandpa suggested quickly. He must have seen the abject disappointment on my face. Sadly, that wasn't what I needed. "Speaking of which, would you like a piece?"

He rose to his feet, opened the tallest drawer, and pulled out my favorite candy, just like old times. How long had it been since I last got a piece of candy from Grandpa? This version of him even kept it in the same place! Two years ago, that drawer felt like it was miles above me, but now that I was taller, it might be just barely within my reach.

I popped the candy into my mouth and savored its sweetness for the first time in years. That was when it occurred to me: as different as this world was, it still shared some commonalities with mine. And if *this* Grandpa kept his candy in the same spot, then perhaps he had the same mindset as *my* Grandpa...

"Hey, Grandpa?"

"Hrmm?"

"The reason I asked about the treasure chest is...my daddy gave me one. Except he hid the key somewhere and told me to try to find it. So I was wondering, if you were in his shoes, where would *you* hide your key?"

In this world, I lived with my dad, so I came up with this cover story. If this Grandpa had the same ideas as mine, then perhaps he could give me a hint that would help me find the key back in my world.

"Well now, that sounds fun!" Grandpa laughed, then started to consider it. "There are two ways to hide something: one for when you don't want it to be found, and one for when you secretly do. If it's a treasure hunt, that would suggest the latter..."

"Yeah, I think he wants me to find it. Why else would he give me the treasure chest?"

"Yes, that sounds right. Smart boy, Koyomi! In that case, if I was the one who gave it to you, and I hid the key hoping for you to find it..." He paused for a moment, then arrived at his answer. "I think I'd choose a spot I know for a fact you'd find in the future, even if you couldn't see it right this moment. That sounds fitting."

"Like where?" I asked.

"Well, I don't know what your dad's house is like..."

"No, *this* house! Where would you hide it around here?"

"This house? Hmmm, good question..."

Ultimately, Grandpa couldn't think of an answer to my most crucial question. This was a big house, so there were probably tons of hiding spots. But then his tone dropped suddenly.

"That reminds me how Yuno used to hide my shoes, that little rascal."

This came as a surprise to me. As far as I knew, Yuno *never* misbehaved like that. Then I remembered: *right, this is a parallel world.* The Yuno here differed from mine. Also, since this world's version of me didn't live here, it was probably a good idea to act as though I hadn't seen her in a while.

"Has she been having fun?" I asked.

Grandpa smiled. "Oh, I'm sure heaven is *lots* of fun."

At this, I very nearly screamed. *Heaven?* This world's Yuno... was dead?

"You know, I adopted her back when you were born."

He started to tell me a story I'd heard countless times before, along with a famous poem that I could practically recite offhand.

"*When you have a child, get a dog.*

In infancy, a guardian;

In childhood, a playmate;

In adolescence, a shoulder to cry on;
And in adulthood, with its death, the value of a life.'

Koyomi, you must be strong and selfless, just like Yuno always was."

Grandpa had adopted her just for me, even though I rarely ever came to visit. And the same was true in this world.

"She really used to hide your shoes...?"

"Oh, you bet. When she was a puppy, she got into all sorts of mischief."

"But then she stopped when she got older?"

"Yes, because I disciplined her. An untrained dog could bite, and I didn't want any tragic accidents."

At long last, I finally understood.

All this time, I assumed Grandpa was an unfeeling monster who hated my guts. But his scolding was never motivated by hate. When he took away my airsoft gun, it was only because I was too young. He just didn't want any accidents—he didn't want me to get hurt! And if this world's version of me got an airsoft gun at age eight, then this Grandpa would surely have done the same.

In both worlds, he always loved me!

"...I miss Yuno..."

I wanted to go back to my world. Here, Grandpa was still alive, but Yuno was gone. In my world, Yuno was still alive, but Grandpa was gone.

"Sadly, you won't be seeing her for quite a while. But I might get to see her myself sometime soon," Grandpa joked...and I understood what he meant.

If this parallel world shared a lot of commonalities with mine, then maybe he had the same illness *my* Grandpa did. Maybe he didn't have a lot of time left. And after I got back home, maybe Yuno's time would run out too. Then they'd both be truly gone... and I'd have no way to see either of them.

Belatedly, I felt the grief of Grandpa's passing rise inside me, and for once, I regretted something that *didn't* involve the treasure chest.

"Hey, Grandpa?"

"Mm?"

"Can I sleep in here with you tonight?" I asked.

"Oh! Why, of course you can, my boy!"

When I saw the way his eyes crinkled with pure delight, for some reason my heart ached even harder—but I choked it down. "Also, can I have another piece of candy?"

"No. You only get one per day."

Oddly, his reply came as a relief, and I laughed. He really was the same guy. And that night, as I drifted off to sleep next to him, I suddenly realized I might know *exactly* where he'd hidden that key.

• • •

The next morning, I awoke to find myself lying in bed with... *Mom*?!

"Whoa!"

"Nnh...? You awake, Koyomi...?" she murmured, rubbing her eyes.

Clearly, *she* didn't find it strange that we were sleeping together—even though it had been a good two years since I started sleeping on my own. Naturally, Grandpa was nowhere to be seen... which probably meant...

"Um...how's Grandpa doing?" I asked timidly.

She opened her eyes wide, then smiled softly and stroked my hair. "The funeral home got him all cleaned up, and now he's resting in the altar room."

Sure enough, I was back in my world, where for some reason I had chosen to sleep in bed with Mom. *How was that possible when I was away in that parallel world?*

"Hey, uh, Mommy? About last night..."

"Aww, don't tell me you're embarrassed! You really needed Mommy to comfort you last night."

Now I understood. While I was off in a world where I had chosen Dad, that version of me was *here*, in the world where I'd chosen Mom. He must have gone crying to her... Now I kinda regretted not talking to Dad while I was over there. Considering it was a world where he and I lived together, we were probably a lot closer there than we were in mine.

How had my parallel self felt when he found out Grandpa had passed away?

"Mommy always thought you hated Grandpa, but that wasn't really true, was it?"

Perhaps this was the answer to that question.

• • •

For the first time in years, I voluntarily paid a visit to Grandpa's room. Two years ago, I would come here once a day to get a piece of candy, but after I decided I hated him, I only ever went when I was forced to. It was practically identical to his room in the other world; even the chest of drawers with the candy inside was the exact same size and shape, and in the same spot.

Did he keep buying candy after I stopped asking for it? I suspected I knew the answer. In fact, I was *sure* the candy was there. After all, he asked me if I wanted a piece the same day he gave me the treasure chest. I regretted turning him down now. I should have just taken it—it was probably my one chance to patch things up with him.

I walked up to the biggest chest of drawers. The top drawer used to be beyond my reach, but now I was tall enough to open it on my own. After all, I was turning ten soon.

I reached up to the drawer where Grandpa used to keep his candy and pulled it open. And sure enough...there they were. My favorite candies in the whole world.

"I'll only take one, Grandpa."

I put a single piece of candy in my mouth, and the familiar sweetness danced on my tongue. But that wasn't what I was really after. I reached deep into the candy bag and felt around...

"...Aha!"

My fingers brushed something cold and hard. I pulled it out, and sure enough, it was a key.

"I knew it..."

I thought back to what parallel Grandpa had said to me.

CHILDHOOD

"I'd choose a spot I know for a fact you'd find in the future, even if you couldn't see it right this moment."

When he first gave me the treasure chest, I despised him and avoided his bedroom. But he had faith that one day, I'd come back for a piece of candy. And even if he was already gone by then, he knew that eventually I'd grow tall enough to open the drawer on my own. And that was precisely where he hid the key.

I went into my room and retrieved the treasure chest from its secret spot. I brought it and the key to the family altar room where my grandfather's body was resting on a futon. I had anticipated that his face would be ashen like a ghost's, but in reality, it was just a bit yellow. That being said, while he was always a lanky man, now he looked downright skeletal. I could scarcely recognize him as the same monster I had feared the past two years.

My grandpa was dead. Never again would he get angry at me... and never again would he give me a piece of candy. Suddenly, I was terrified. I hadn't actually *talked* to him since the day he gave me the treasure chest.

"Grandpa?" As I called out to him, my eyes suddenly filled with tears. "I'm gonna open the treasure chest, okay?" Before my tears could fall, I plunged the key into the keyhole.

There was a light *click*...and the lid opened.

"Oh...!"

Inside was an airsoft gun labeled *Ages 10 & Up.*

"It's the same one..."

The one I begged Dad to buy me when I was eight. The one Grandpa confiscated because I was too young. The whole reason

I stopped liking him. At the time I was sure he threw it away, but instead, he held onto it.

Packed with the airsoft gun was a scrap of paper, folded in half. I opened it to find a message written in shaky handwriting, far worse than my own.

Happy 10th birthday, Koyomi. Don't forget: never point it at anyone.

Outside, I could hear Yuno barking.

Interlude

T HAT WAS MY FIRST EXPERIENCE with parallel worlds.
Incidentally, Yuno surpassed my expectations by surviving
another two years after that. She died peacefully in her sleep.

Looking back, it was around then that the world rapidly
began to acknowledge the concept of parallel worlds as well. It
was Japan's own Imaginary Science Research Institute that first
officially proved their existence. That's right—the same place
where Dad worked.

To summarize it:

*Our world is linked to dozens of alternate worlds that we un-
consciously visit on a regular basis. The physical form does not travel,
but rather, the consciousness is transplanted into another version of
the self that exists within the parallel world. The process happens
instantaneously, with no time lag.*

*The closer the world is to our own, the smaller the differences
between the two. Often, it's something as trivial as what we had for*

breakfast that morning. Furthermore, the closer the parallel world is to ours, the more likely we will travel there without realizing it, and the shorter the visit will be. This is why we don't notice when it happens. It is this phenomenon that results in "misremembered" times and dates for social gatherings, or "misplaced" belongings that turn up in unexpected places.

It is believed that on rare occasions, humans may travel to more distant worlds that are dramatically different from our own. In those cases, the individual will feel as though they walked into an alternate reality.

Henceforth, the act of traveling between parallel worlds will be referred to as "parallel shifting."

As you might expect, the announcement was treated as a joke at first. But then Professor Satou Itoko, director of the Imaginary Science Research Institute, began to substantiate her claims with the data she'd amassed through her research. In doing so, she sparked unprecedented levels of debate. Scientific organizations across the globe came together to try to verify (or debunk) this lofty claim. And just three short years later, each and every international scientific authority confirmed the ISRI's findings. Imaginary science was now an accepted field of study.

Then, right before I turned fifteen, they developed a device that could measure IP—short for Imaginary Elements Print, the signifier unique to each parallel world. Scholars from every field were given prototypes as part of a trial run. This function would come to be known as an IEPP counter.

From that point in time forward, children were affixed with IP bands right from birth—wearable devices with an IEPP counter installed. At the time of birth, the software registered the current world as World Zero, and by continually monitoring your IP against that initial value, you could determine which world you were in at any given time. With this innovation, society quickly accepted parallel worlds as a part of everyday life.

That being said, back when I was fifteen, there were a lot of skeptics who only saw parallel worlds as a fictional concept. Even long after it was recognized as a valid field of study, some people still treated it as a pseudoscience.

As for me, while the world was rapidly shifting to accommodate a new relationship with imaginary science, an earthshaking event would soon change *my* world. And it, too, involved parallel worlds.

That being said, it was a highly unusual case...

To Every You
I've Loved Before

CHAPTER 2

Adolescence

Never in my life had I studied for a test before. Not to blow my own horn, but it quickly became apparent that I was smarter—*much* smarter—than my peers at school. I never needed to go over my textbooks to keep up with my classes, and in elementary school, I got perfect scores on all my tests. Of course, in junior and high school, those same perfect scores were a little harder to come by, but I still never scored lower than a 90. As a result, in junior high, I developed a superiority complex and decided everyone else at my school was an idiot.

Naturally, I paid a steep price for my childish ignorance. Although I intended to conceal my condescension, it seeped from my every pore, and to be quite frank, it cost me every friendship I could've otherwise had. But I was fine with that—or at least, I tried to pretend I was—so I started choosing solitude of my own volition.

Unfortunately, I craved social interaction by nature, and as my time at junior high came to an end, I strongly regretted the way I'd spent it. While pretending to read a book between classes, I would eavesdrop on my classmates and hear them excitedly talking about throwing a graduation party and going to karaoke afterwards. Obviously, I wasn't invited. Through my body language exuded an aura of "spare me your stupidity," on the inside, I was painfully jealous.

Then graduation day rolled around. While everyone else was signing each other's yearbooks, I just went home. And when I got there, I frowned down at my blank yearbook and made a promise to myself. *I'll make friends in high school!*

The high school I enrolled at was the most competitive one in our entire prefecture. Suffice it to say, no one from my junior high class made it in with me. I was therefore starting over with a clean slate. On top of that, since everyone in my class would likely be just as smart as me, I could build genuine connections without looking down on them...right?

The entrance exam was held four days after I graduated from junior high. While I knew it would be a challenging test, I was sure I could get perfect marks in every subject as long as I studied hard beforehand. But...if I *did* get a perfect score, the other students would find me intimidating, and then I'd be ostracized again... Therefore, I decided not to study for the test whatsoever. I was confident I'd still pass. And sure enough, I did.

Then one day, a week before the entrance ceremony, the school called and asked me if I would speak at the ceremony as the class valedictorian. When I asked why, the answer was simple: despite not having studied, I had *still* scored the highest of all the applicants. They said I was free to decline, so...I said no. By announcing myself as the valedictorian, everyone would know I got the highest score on the test. I thought it might damage my chances of making friends. (At the time, I was still seriously convinced that it was my *intelligence* that drove people away from me.)

Having successfully declined the title, I walked into the entrance ceremony like any other student. The valedictorian speech was instead given by some girl with glasses, and later I would learn that the task had fallen to the second-highest scorer.

Little did I know, however, that declining the title of valedictorian would have a massive effect on my life. Sure, there were probably parallel worlds where I agreed to it, but every now and then, I still wondered... Were those versions of me any happier for it?

• • •

Sadly, that modest dream of mine—to make friends in high school—crashed and burned not even a month in.

In the beginning, I really tried. I took the initiative and struck up conversations with other students while trying not to seem weird. But once again, my grades got in the way.

Because our high school was the top-ranked school in Oita Prefecture, classes were organized based on our test scores. As the top scorer, I was naturally assigned to Class A, where students seemed to care more about studying and good grades than they did about having fun with friends. In the beginning, I started to think maybe I should have answered some questions wrong on purpose so they would have put me in a lower class.

Class A was full of students who spent every minute of free time studying or going to cram school. I got the feeling that the mere *suggestion* of going somewhere for fun would earn me funny looks, so I didn't bother. But as I watched them, it dawned on me.

For as hard as they all work, they're still worse than me—and I don't even try.

The instant that thought occurred to me, it was all over. I was already judging them the same way I judged my peers in junior high. Having lost all academic drive, I started getting bad grades on purpose. 97, 89, 83, 79, 73... But even then, I was *still* somehow in the upper percentile of test takers.

I officially had no way of making friends. Despite being so academically focused, Class A had still managed to form little cliques within it, without me. And so, just like junior high, I spent my days alone with my nose in a book.

But the *real* story began one summer day after school...

• • •

"Koyomi!"

At first, I didn't realize someone was calling my name. After all, my entire high school career had consisted of me walking these halls alone. On the occasion someone was forced to address me, it was by my surname, Takasaki. It simply wasn't within the realm of expectation for a female student I barely knew to call me by my first name.

So, my brain processed it as background noise while I packed my bag and got ready to leave the room.

"Hey!"

When she grabbed my arm, however, it obviously snapped me to attention. Startled, I turned around.

"What are you ignoring me for?" she asked.

I...didn't understand. The classmate currently scowling at me with her hand on my arm was none other than Takigawa Kazune. She was a bespectacled girl with long dark hair tied up in a ponytail. She was a brilliant student whose test scores trounced the rest of Class A—and incidentally, she was the same girl who had inherited the title of valedictorian after I passed on it.

But while we were in the same class, we had never so much as *spoken* to one another, not even once. We were never partners on any school projects, and we never said each other's names— *especially* not first names.

Confused, I just stared blankly back at her. I must have looked like a total idiot because her scowl deepened.

"Why are you looking at me like that? You're not still hung up on what happened, are you? Because I'm not mad at you anymore."

I was truly, utterly clueless. What was she talking about? What happened? Why was she mad? My mind was awash with a thousand questions.

"Let's just walk home together, okay? We can talk it out on the way."

With that, she took me by the hand and started to leave the classroom. I should have been elated to hold hands with a girl, but instead I was *terrified*.

"Um... Takigawa-san...?" Too cowardly to shake her off, I timidly called out to the back of her head.

She stopped walking and looked back at me. "What did you just call me?! Even if you're unhappy with me, that's no excuse to get passive-aggressive!"

"What? I'm not! What should I call you, then?"

"Are you mad at me now?" she asked.

This conversation just wasn't making sense! Maybe this girl had crammed her brain so full of knowledge that it broke something else. Meanwhile, our classmates were staring at us.

Even though I'd given up on making friends with anyone, I still didn't want to be seen as weird. "Look, just...let go of me, okay?"

Surprisingly, she did as I asked without complaint. Her hand was much warmer than the expression on her face, and I was startled to find that I missed it as soon as it was gone. But I didn't have time to think about that right now.

"What's gotten into you, Takigawa-san?" I asked.

"I should ask *you* the same thing, Koyomi! Something's going on with you! I know we've had a few misunderstandings lately, but normally you'd never—"

And with that, Takigawa-san gasped as some sort of realization hit her. She looked down at the watch on her left wrist, inhaled sharply, and looked back up at me to say something—but no words came.

She was silent for about five seconds, and then... "I'm sorry."

With that, she hurried out of the room like it was on fire.

Given that the whole class was now staring at me, clearly they *did* have other interests besides just studying...but at that point, I didn't care anymore.

By the time I stepped out into the hall, Takigawa-san was already long gone.

• • •

Takigawa Kazune, queen geek. A fitting title if I ever heard one. She wore her waist-length hair in a ponytail, and barely concealed behind her coke-bottle lenses were a pair of sharp eyes that kept others at bay. We were three months into our first year of high school and she never once got anything less than the top score on her tests. I had also never seen her interact with any of the other students.

So what was all *that* about?

I thought about it all night after I got home from school, but I really couldn't remember ever talking to her before. In fact, I was pretty sure we never even made eye contact. So it went without saying that we were in no position to get into an argument, much less call each other by our first names. Maybe she mistook me for someone else...? No, she unmistakably said *Koyomi*. She was definitely talking to me.

I glanced over at her desk, sitting in the northwest corner of the classroom. My desk was near the center, so I could only see her from an angle. She was sitting up straight, facing forward, and listening to the lesson with narrowed eyes. But when I paused to observe her, I realized she was hardly taking any notes. Sure, she'd scribble down a few words on occasion, but she certainly wasn't copying down the chalkboard verbatim. And neither was I.

After that class came a ten-minute break period. As I prepped for the next lesson, I kept glancing at Takigawa-san. She didn't look my way even once. The way she read her book exuded such unapproachable vibes that I was half-convinced what happened yesterday was all a dream or something.

But every now and then, a fellow classmate would look from me to her and back again. I knew they had to be wondering what was going on between us. If any of them were friends with me, they'd be asking me a thousand questions right about now...so ironically enough, for once in my life, I was grateful to be alone. *I* wanted to be the one asking a thousand questions—though admittedly, I did have *one* little theory.

As a result, I spent the day spying on Takigawa-san, but she didn't look at me once all day. I thought about saying something to her on my way out after school, but she moved so quickly that I could only watch her disappear into the distance.

Then again, if my suspicions were right, I didn't really need to worry about it...or so I told myself.

However, when I opened my shoe locker, I found a folded scrap of paper inside.

Huh? I immediately opened it and read it on the spot.

It was a note from Takigawa-san.

• • •

"Welcome! Room for one?"

"Oh, uh, I'm supposed to meet someone here..."

"Could I get their name?"

"Takigawa."

"Takigawa... Yes, here it is. Room 301. Elevator's right over there."

Prompted by the employee, I boarded the elevator and took it to the third floor.

This karaoke lounge was about a fifteen-minute walk away from the train station. Due to the distance and the slightly inflated prices, people my age didn't really come here. Even so, the rooms were well-kept, and the food was good, so it was popular with adults, or so my mom told me.

When I arrived at the third floor, I quickly found Room 301. I put my hand on the knob and took a deep breath... And summoned my courage... And finally opened the door.

No one was inside.

Upon further inspection, I could see a schoolbag sitting on the table, so clearly she had to be around here somewhere. Maybe she was using the restroom? Finding no one inside took the wind completely out of my sails. *What now? Do I sit and wait for her to get back? Or should I stand outside and—*

"Takasaki-kun?"

"Aaagh!" I cried. The sudden voice behind me made me stumble forward into the room.

"Er... Are you all right?" It was Takigawa-san, and contrary to her words, she didn't sound all too concerned about my well-being. She stared down at me as she held a drink in one hand.

"Yeah, uh, I'm fine."

"I was just grabbing a drink. They're free, you know. Would you like to go get one? You can use one of the glasses there."

And so, at her prompting, I went to get a free drink on my own. I dropped in three ice cubes and filled my glass with ginger ale. Over the short walk back to the private room, I eased my fraught nerves.

Wait a minute—she called me Takasaki-kun this time! Before yesterday, that would have felt normal, but after she called me Koyomi, well... Anyway, she had expressly invited me to a place where we were all but guaranteed not to encounter anyone from our school. Surely she was going to give me *some* sort of explanation for all this—though I suspected I already knew what it was. Nervous and hopeful, I pushed the door open once more.

She was sitting up straight, just as she did in class, and was sipping her iced tea through a straw. I sat down across from her and took a sip of my ginger ale.

Awkward.

Was I supposed to initiate the conversation here? No, if anyone ought to talk, it was her! She didn't *actually* invite me here to sing, right? And yet she remained silent. The only thing holding me together right now was the muffled sound of the latest pop single over the speakers.

But when the song ended, and the room went quiet...

"I'm sorry about yesterday," Takigawa-san apologized, her expression unchanged.

"Oh, uh... No, it's fine..." I stammered.

"You must have been so confused."

"Yeah, uh... What was that about?" I asked.

Instead of answering, she raised her wristwatch up for me to see. "Do you know what this is?"

"It's...not a watch?" I asked, though I suspected I had an answer for that too. On the small LCD screen were just three digits, while an ordinary wristwatch would have had four.

"No, it's not. It's an IP band. Have you heard of them?"

Sure enough, it was exactly what I expected. The field of imaginary science had developed rapidly over the past few years, and IP bands were one of the latest innovations it had produced. With your home world registered as 000, you could check your IP number to see how far you were from home at any given time. IP bands were still in the refining stage, so only scholars and their families were given prototypes to test out. I didn't have one, but my dad showed me his before. It looked exactly like the one she was wearing.

"Yeah, I know of them."

"Okay then, so I guess you know what this number means."

She pointed to her three-digit number: 085.

That would suggest...

"The Takigawa-san I spoke to yesterday was a parallel one from 85 worlds away?!" I exclaimed.

"Yep. And I'm still here, it seems. But I didn't realize I shifted, so I spoke to you like you were the same Koyomi from back home."

"So you're saying...back in *your* World Zero, you address me by my first name?"

She was certainly implying as much. What kind of relationship did we have in *her* universe?

"Well...the Koyomi *I* know is more of a social butterfly, but I suppose when you parallel shift across 85 worlds, these things can turn out rather differently."

When I first started high school, I promised myself I would be more outgoing. In the beginning, I did make a conscious effort to be friendly and initiate conversations. But ultimately, I went right back to being the same loner I always was. Had this parallel me 85 worlds away succeeded where I failed? Did he have lots of friends who all called him by his first name?

"Does that mean...in your world, you and I are friends?"

At this, her brow furrowed slightly. She was fairly hard to read in general, but in this case, I could tell she didn't like the question. Averting her eyes, she muttered, "Well, to be completely transparent...we're dating."

...What?

Did she just respond to "Are we friends?" *with...*"We're dating"*?
DATING?*

"Wh-what...? Dating, as in...you, and me? We're...like...boyfriend and girlfriend...? Or whatever?" I stammered, flustered.

She narrowed her eyes even further, glaring at me. On its own, it was pretty intimidating, but it lost a lot of its impact when I noticed her ears had turned red.

"This is completely throwing me off. You're *nothing* like the Koyomi I know!" she yelled.

"Well, I don't know the guy! What's he like?"

"He's *manly*, for one thing!"

I was well aware of my unmanliness, thank you very much, but hearing someone else call it out point-blank really stung.

"Okay, well... Like you said, people's personalities are bound to be different when you shift eighty-five worlds away. I mean... there's no way you and I could ever...you know...be in that kind of relationship in my world!"

"What relationship *do* you have with her?" she asked.

"We've never even talked before. Until yesterday, I mean," I admitted.

"No wonder you were confused."

"Darn right I was! If you have an IP band, why didn't you think to check it first?"

"Normally I only ever shift by one or two worlds, not *eighty-five*!" she shot back. "And I hardly ever notice the difference most times, so I don't think to check!"

To be fair, I could understand where she was coming from. Imaginary science was progressing so rapidly. There were new theories and discoveries being reported practically every day. Because of that, even the average member of society had a baseline understanding of parallel worlds.

These alternate universes were said to be countless, all of them overlapping with one another and in constant flux. As a result, human beings shifted between the closest ones on a near-daily basis. But because worlds close in proximity were nearly identical, most people wouldn't notice they shifted at all.

For instance, suppose you put an eraser in a drawer in your home world, but when you went to fetch it, it was inexplicably missing. You were *so* sure you put it there, too. However, then you went and opened the next drawer and found it there instead. You'd be confused, but nonetheless take the eraser and go about your day.

This situation would indicate that you had inadvertently left your home world at some point between the moment you put your eraser away and the moment you went to retrieve it. Here in this *other* world, your *other* self put their eraser in the second drawer instead of the first. This inadvertent movement between parallel worlds was now known as parallel shifting—the theoretical culprit behind tons of mundane misunderstandings.

As I understood it, minor shifts didn't significantly impact daily life, but a long-distance shift could create severe confusion and palpably feel like an "alternate universe" for the affected person. That said, major shifts were incredibly rare, and as such, most people could go their whole lives blissfully unaware that they ever shifted at all.

For better or for worse, I myself had experienced a long-distance shift once before. Back when my grandpa died, I some-how shifted to a world where he was still alive. I had no clue how many worlds away it was, but fortunately, I woke up back in World Zero the next morning without incident. And because of that experience, I readily believed Takigawa-san was telling the truth.

"Anyway, I think it's all cleared up now. Hope you get home soon."

"Yeah," she replied simply.

Silence. She took another sip through her straw, and I downed my ginger ale—I liked it best when it was a little watered down. But by the time our glasses were empty, she still hadn't spoken again.

Personally, there was something I was dying to ask. *How the hell did my 85th self end up in a relationship with her?* Despite her good looks, she always struck me as a rude and pessimistic person...but after seeing her blush over the word "dating," I was starting to find her cute. Being a teenage guy with a healthy interest in such things, I couldn't help but get some ideas. *Hey, if the other me had a shot, then maybe I do too.* That being said, I didn't have the balls to actually ask her.

"Well, uh, I'm gonna get going now," I said.

Grabbing my bookbag, I rose to my feet. As far as I was concerned, now that I understood what happened yesterday and she apologized for it, this conversation was over. Soon, she would go back home to World 85, and I'd go back to having nothing to do with this version of her. This was just an anomaly.

But right as I grabbed the bulky doorknob—

"Wait," I heard her say in a tiny voice behind me.

She had spoken just as the knob rattled loudly in my hand, and I suspected it was her way of giving me the option to ignore it. I stopped and closed the door again. If I were to be completely honest...I didn't want this anomaly to end just yet.

"What is it?" I turned back slowly.

She stared down at her still-empty glass, straw in her mouth, carefully avoiding my gaze. "You *are* technically Takasaki Koyomi, right?"

Technically? From my perspective, I was the *only* Takasaki Koyomi. "That's me."

"Then you know what he's thinking, right?" she asked.

"...I mean, I know what *I'm* thinking..."

"Yes, and you're Takasaki Koyomi," she said again.

"Well, yeah...technically." *Ugh, now she's got* me *saying it!*

"Then help me, would you? I don't understand the way he thinks... And at this rate, we might break up soon."

It was a bizarre request. What should I do when my other self's relationship wasn't going well? What advice could I offer? Unlike him, I'd never *had* a girlfriend.

"We keep having these misunderstandings, and it feels like we're fighting..." she began.

"Wait, uh, slow down a sec," I cut in.

Loath though I was to admit it, I once read a romantic advice column—not that I was expressly searching for it, I assure you; I just randomly saw it online and accidentally clicked on it, and I was really bored at the time, so I lightly skimmed over it—that warned never to interrupt a girl while she was talking. But...I probably didn't need to worry about that right now, since she was technically already dating me.

"What is it?"

"I just, uh, wanna make sure real quick: you're Takigawa Kazune-san, right?" I asked.

"That's right."

"High school first-year?"

"Yes," she said.

"In my world, it's July—three months since school started back in April. What about yours?"

"It's the exact same. There's never any time lag when parallel shifting—didn't you know that?"

"Yeah, I know. Okay then, did you and I go to the same elementary or junior high?" I asked.

"No..."

"So we met for the first time here in high school?"

"Correct."

That was everything I wanted to double-check...but the conclusion it led me to was unfathomable. I mean, I *understood* it, but I didn't accept it—didn't *want* to accept it.

"So you're saying that...over the course of the three months since we've met, you and I started dating, now it's going poorly, and we might break up?"

"Two months. We started dating in May," she answered matter-of-factly.

Wasn't that moving a little too quickly? Or was I just an old-fashioned prude? "Um... Could I ask you how the two of you got together?"

Now I'd gone and asked the big question. But eh, it felt like the right moment, and since it was 85 entire worlds away from here, it was basically all fanfiction to me, anyway.

"I'm not sure how it went in this world, but in mine, right after the school year started, the whole class decided to go out to karaoke as an icebreaker."

"What? Our class?"

"Yeah."

"Unbelievable."

"Not everyone showed up, obviously, but I'd say about half of the class did, including me and Koyomi. But then it got late, and someone even brought in alcohol. I didn't want to get in trouble if we were caught, so I snuck out by myself."

Compared to scolding them or joining in, that was possibly the smartest choice.

"Then, as I was walking downtown, some weirdo started harassing me," she said.

"What kind of weirdo?"

"He was dressed in dirty clothes and wearing sunglasses at night. He kept following me, asking me if I wanted to buy... something, I don't know what. I tried to ignore him, but then out of the blue, he grabbed my arm and tried to drag me into an alley."

"Scary," I commented, like I was watching a crime report on TV.

Hard to believe there were any genuinely dangerous people in a city as rural as ours.

"But then, Koyomi rescued me."

"What...?" For a second, this didn't process.

"Before I could scream, he came charging into the alley. Then he tackled the weirdo, grabbed my hand, and took off running. We ran all the way to a busy area, and once we caught our breath... that was when I realized who saved me. When I asked him why, he said he noticed my absence, and since it was late, he followed me out so he could walk me home. Then he laughed about how he totally made the right call."

"He who?" I asked.

"Takasaki Koyomi."

"You've gotta be kidding me..."

Granted, we were an entire 85 worlds apart, but I could absolutely *never* see myself doing something that badass and manly. Otherwise, I had no excuse for being the pathetic nerd I was now.

Please, tell me you're joking!

"I'm serious."

Damn it!

"That was at the end of April... At the beginning of May, I asked him out."

"You asked him out?" I asked.

"Yes."

"Him, as in...?"

"Koyomi," she confirmed.

Nope. Couldn't be a parallel of *my* world. At this point, this was like a straight-up isekai story.

"He said yes right away, but..."

Her tone went dark, and when I glanced over at her, I saw that the girl who was gleefully gushing about her boyfriend's bravery just moments prior was now looking much gloomier. *After that classic rom-com start to their relationship, how could it possibly be going poorly?*

This other Takasaki Koyomi must have revealed his true colors. He probably only saved her purely by happenstance, and now she was starting to see just what a loser he actually was. That was the *real* Takasaki Koyomi. Sad, I know.

"But now things aren't going well, you said? How come?" I wasn't entirely sure I wanted to hear the answer, but I needed to keep the conversation rolling.

"He's always hanging out with other girls. And when I ask why, he said it'd be silly to stop hanging out with his friends just because he has a girlfriend."

Nope. Couldn't be me. Who the hell was this guy?

She continued. "I said, 'Well, could you at least not hang out with them one-on-one?' But he was like, 'It's not cheating!' So he tells these girls that he has a girlfriend, and then he tells me whenever he hangs out with them... I just don't get it. It'd make more sense to me if he was hiding it."

No kidding. I didn't get it either.

"Look, you're Takasaki Koyomi, right?"

"Yeah..."

"Tell me, what in the world is he thinking?"

I wanted to ask him that myself! At this point, all I had to rely on was that *other* advice column I randomly saw online and clicked on by accident and only read because I was bored—*Ladies Tell All: Why Do Men Cheat?*

"Well, uh... No matter how much you may love...*curry*, for instance, if you eat it every single day, you'll get sick of it, you know...? But if it's your favorite, then you'll always come back to it, so, um... They say a woman's strongest skill is her patience..." I rambled out.

"How very pedestrian."

In the same way that I was struggling to believe *her* boyfriend was really Takasaki Koyomi, I was starting to question whether *this* lovestruck damsel was really Takigawa Kazune.

However, her icy glare was exactly like the Takigawa-san I knew. "Well... Maybe you're right."

"Huh?"

"Maybe he *is* sick of 'curry' every day."

"That, or...maybe he just treats his female friends the same as his male friends?" I suggested.

"What?"

I couldn't possibly imagine what some fanfiction version of me was thinking. But I *was* technically Takasaki Koyomi, so... maybe it was up to me to cheer her up a bit.

"Well...based on what you've told me, it seems like the other me hangs out with girls whether or not he's dating them—same as with his bros. I bet they're all in the 'friend' category. And the... you know, *romantic* stuff he wants to do with you because you're his girlfriend—he probably doesn't think of anyone else that way at all, so he can probably hang out with them like normal without it being weird... Maybe?" That was the best I could manage entirely off the cuff.

"...Is that how it is for you?" she asked.

No, I don't have *friends.* But obviously I couldn't tell her that. "Yeah, more or less."

"I see."

It was just a little white lie, though I had no way of knowing if it actually helped. She averted her eyes and went quiet once more. But as she gazed at her empty glass, it seemed as though her expression was just a bit brighter.

Likewise, I sat there in silence. At times like these, it would have been helpful if a love song was playing in the background, but instead, some old guy was crooning a sad enka ballad about drowning his sorrows in whiskey. If only I was old enough to drink.

"You can leave now, if you like," I heard her say.

Part of me wanted to stay, but I shook the thought away and rose to my feet. *Don't get it twisted. She's not* your *girlfriend. The Takasaki Koyomi she loves isn't you.*

"Okay then, I'm gonna head out," I said.

"Oh, and you don't owe me anything. I'll pay for the room."

"You sure?"

"My family's rich, so I have a lot of spending money."

"Yeah, but that money belongs to this world's Takigawa-san. You shouldn't use it without her permission."

"What? Oh, you're right. I suppose I shouldn't..."

Her eyes widened like she was caught off-guard. It was adorable, but I chose to disregard this observation. Otherwise it would add fuel to a flame I didn't want burning.

"Are you leaving too?"

"No, I think I'll stay and sing a little before I go."

"Oh, so you actually *like* karaoke?"

"What are you talking about? Don't you remember all those times we— Oh." She hung her head guiltily, though in my opinion she'd done nothing wrong. If anything, the reminder that she wasn't from this world would help me stay in mine. "...Would you like to sing something?"

"Nah, I'm going home. See you." Once again, I turned that bulky knob—

"Thank you, Takasaki-kun."

I froze in place.

"Since there's a chance I won't see you again...I just wanted to let you know I appreciate it," she said. "Because of you, I feel a little better now, so...thanks."

Without saying a word in return, I opened the door and walked out.

It was the coolest moment of my entire life, if I do say so myself.

• • •

The next day, after making the best possible exit at the karaoke lounge...I was back at the karaoke lounge. With Takigawa-san. Again.

When I tried peeking at her in class, I couldn't really tell if she was the girl from World 85 or not. I was curious to know if she made it back home, but I didn't have the balls to talk to her. When I opened my shoe locker after school, however, I found another note from her waiting for me.

Sadly, the second go around was still nerve-racking for me. I doused my parched throat with another free drink and decided to try to get the ball rolling. "Uhh... Hi...?"

"Hello."

Which Takigawa-san *was* this? I seriously couldn't tell. Was she from World Zero or World 85? Given that she used the same strategy to get me here, my guess was the latter, but even then I couldn't be certain.

"You're the parallel Takigawa-san...right?"

"Yes," she replied.

"I see you haven't gone home yet."

"Well, the greater the distance between two worlds, the more difficult parallel shifting becomes. And since we're 85 worlds apart, I imagine it'll take a lot longer than a day or two."

Her matter-of-fact tone gave me pause. "You knew that the whole time?"

"Yes...?"

"Then why did you say you weren't going to see me again?" I asked.

"I said there was a *chance* I wouldn't."

"...Oh."

"Please don't be upset. I've never gone through this before, so I don't know for sure how long it usually takes. There *was* a small chance I wouldn't see you again after that. I was just reasonably certain it wouldn't happen that fast."

Her argument was bulletproof, but frankly, I didn't care about winning this one. I was just a tiny bit glad to see her again. "Okay, so why did you invite me here again?"

"Well, you're the only one I can hang out with in this world!"

At that, my heart fluttered. "You wanted to *hang out*? Not just talk about parallel worlds?"

"Oh, we could do that. How much do you know about imaginary science?"

Full disclosure: my dad had a fairly prestigious position at the Imaginary Science Research Institute. He liked to tell me about his work. Honestly, I was pretty sure I knew more about imaginary science than most people my age.

"Eh... I know a little."

I chose to undersell myself on purpose. That said, I went with "I know a little" rather than my usual "I don't know much," purely out of respect for her intelligence.

"A little, you say... Then let's have an imaginary science quiz."

Oh god, what?

"Question one: What does the 'IP' stand for in 'IP band'?"

"Uhhh... Imaginary Print," I replied.

"Close. You forgot 'Elements.' Question two: What is imaginary space likened to?"

"The ocean?"

"Correct. Question three: What is the name of the world's foremost imaginary science expert?"

"What? How should I know?"

"Bzzzt. Her name is Satou Itoko. Question four..."

And so she spent the whole time quizzing me on imaginary science. She seemed impressed with my level of knowledge, and her questions became more and more esoteric over time. I found it kind of fun to try to answer them.

Like yesterday, I was the first to leave, but this time I didn't try to act cool. It'd only get more cringey the more I kept doing it.

And as for the question of when she would shift back home... Well, let me put it this way—a full week later, she was still Takigawa-san 85.

In the beginning, I was confident that she'd go home sooner or later, so I happily hung out with her every day at the karaoke lounge, chatting about imaginary science. As I suspected based on the fact that she had an IP band, her father was involved in the field as well—and when I asked where he worked, it turned out that he and my father were colleagues. And so, flaunting the knowledge we each gleaned from our dads, we had a great time discussing all sorts of topics. Never in my wildest dreams did I think I'd ever have a stimulating conversation with someone the same age as me.

As we chatted, I came to realize just how truly intelligent she was—and not just because of her test scores. You see, whenever I talked to someone, I had a bad habit of subconsciously leaving out details I didn't think were necessary, so people were constantly asking me to back up and explain something. But Takigawa-san was different. She was the first person my age who could actually keep up with me.

But what brought us even closer together was probably the point when we hashed out how to address each other—and it was all because of one particular conversation we were having regarding parallel worlds.

"Oh, I get it. So the version of you in your world—"

"Stop," she said suddenly.

"Huh?"

"Having to say 'the version of you in your world' is too long. It's exhausting!"

Whenever something annoyed her, she always cut straight to the chase. Personally, it was annoying for me too, but when parallel worlds were involved, we needed a way to keep things distinct and clear. After all, if I called both of her selves "Takigawa-san," it would just get confusing.

"Okay then, what should I do? Call you by your numbers?"

"That's even worse. Let's just use surname for one and given name for the other."

"Huh?"

"In *this* world, the two of you are Takasaki-kun and Takigawa-san, but in *my* world, we're Koyomi and Kazune. It makes sense, since that's what we call each other anyway."

"So...you want me to call you Kazune?"

"Sure, why not?"

And so we decided that I'd refer to my 85th self as Koyomi, and the 85th Takigawa-san as Kazune. Conversely, she would call *me* Takasaki-kun, and refer to the Takigawa-san I knew as just that—Takigawa-san. For some reason, it felt really awkward to address a female classmate by her given name only, even though I couldn't explain it.

Every now and then, instead of talking science, we actually sang karaoke instead. Surprisingly, Takigawa-san—er, *Kazune*—was a really good singer. She tore my crappy performances apart and then coached me to sing better. Before I knew it, we were on close enough terms that I was comfortable snapping back at her when she got too pushy.

Then one day, I got so cocky that I flat-out asked her, "Well then, could you date me instead of Koyomi?"

I don't really remember what led to it—we were probably talking about what she would do if she stayed stuck in my world forever. At the time, I really struggled to keep my tone perfectly casual so she wouldn't think I was serious. But perhaps that struggle worked in my favor... No, probably not.

Her eyes turned serious. She said, "To be honest, I'm not attracted to you."

"Exactly, so..." I started to respond promptly in a tone that suggested I had anticipated this answer well before I even asked the question. If I let her see that it hurt me, it was all over.

But even then, Kazune was one step ahead of me.

"But... I really love Koyomi, so...perhaps we could be destined for each other, even 85 entire worlds away. If you're angling for that, you'll have to give it your best."

I was speechless. Was she saying I had a chance with this world's version of her?

Then, I realized something. Despite all the conversations I'd had with Kazune, I still hadn't spoken to Takigawa-san once. What was that version of her even like?

• • •

I was sure Kazune would have gone home by the following Monday, but nope, she was still Kazune.

"How many days has it been?" I asked.

"Exactly one week."

We sat at the table at our usual karaoke lounge as she gave me her status report. By this point, our sunny optimism was fading, and we were both starting to get worried that she'd never shift back.

"So I asked my...*parallel* father about long-distance shifts," she continued.

"What did he say?"

"They're considered to be extremely uncommon, and because there are no proven clinical case studies, little is known about them."

"I see."

"One working theory suggests that long-distance shifts are more common in older people—that it could explain the root cause of dementia. But even then..." she trailed off.

"Yeah, you're way too young for that."

"I'd like to think so, at least!"

Ultimately, we had no clue what to do.

"Well, I do have *one* idea. You could tell him what's going on. Maybe they could scan you at the lab or something?"

She seemingly hadn't told anyone but me she was from a parallel world. Given that she was wearing a prototype IP band, I thought she was probably obligated to report that sort of thing, but whatever.

"I'm considering it as a last resort, but...I just know they'll study me like a lab rat. Ideally, I'd like to go home the natural way, with no one else finding out."

I couldn't really argue with that. Nobody would want to be a laboratory's guinea pig...and besides, I kind of liked being the only person special enough to know the truth.

"After I get home, I'll try asking *my* dad too. Supposedly he's pretty high up the chain of command, so maybe he's heard the latest developments," I said.

"Please do. I'll take whatever sort of hint I can get."

The mood was too gloomy to sing karaoke that night, so we went straight home instead. When I arrived, I immediately called my dad on the phone. His work schedule was erratic, so there was really no guarantee he'd answer, but this time I got lucky.

"Hello?"

"Hey Dad, it's me, Koyomi."

"What's up, kiddo?"

With Dad, I didn't need to waste time making small talk.

Instead I cut to the chase. "I have a question for you. Is it possible to voluntarily shift to a world of your choice?"

In every work of fiction that featured parallel worlds, there was nearly always a way to do just that. Its difficulty varied widely—sometimes it involved specialized machinery, and other times, characters just closed their eyes in the dark and wished for it really hard—but if parallel worlds existed, then a method for voluntary travel was all but certain. Maybe, just maybe, there was a way to send Kazune home again.

In fact, I had an idea of how to achieve it.

Approximately five years prior, when I shifted to a world where my grandpa was still alive, I awoke to find myself in a strange pod-like enclosure at the Imaginary Science Research Institute. Looking back, it seemed so obvious—surely it had to be a machine designed to send people to parallel worlds. Granted, I kept that experience a secret so I couldn't say anything outright, but if my suspicions were correct, it was possible he'd volunteer some sort of information about it.

Unfortunately, the answer he gave was a little vague for my liking.

"Theoretically...yes, it's thought to be possible. In fact, we're researching it at the lab. But right now, we don't have the technology to make it work. I'd say it'll take us another ten years before we get there."

Ten years? No way in hell could we wait that long. But at the very least, this answer *did* seem to confirm my suspicions about that pod.

The very next day, I headed to school, planning to let Kazune know that voluntary shifting was at least theoretically possible. On my way there, however, I happened to spot her on the street up ahead.

Luckily, none of our classmates were around, so I ran up behind her and whispered, "Morning, Kazune."

At that, she whipped her head around to look at me, then jumped back in fear. Her reaction told me everything I needed to know.

Kazune—no, Takigawa-san—hastily looked down at the IP band on her wrist. I couldn't see the number myself, but I suspected it was something small, like 000 or 001. At the very least, it most likely *wasn't* 085 anymore. Kazune had gone back home.

Then, without a word, Takigawa-san turned and dashed off toward campus.

During a shift, the subject switched places with their other self in the parallel world. That meant that Takigawa-san had spent the past week in World 85 with Koyomi. What had they talked about? And now that she was home again, how did she feel about me?

Sad to say, I wasn't yet mature enough to let it all end without trying to find out.

• • •

Three days later, I sat waiting for Takigawa-san at our usual karaoke lounge. I meant to talk to her right away, but it took me three days just to summon the courage to put a note in her shoe locker. My heart raced out of control the whole time I was writing it too. If only we were mutuals on social media, it would have been so much easier. *Gah, I should have asked Kazune if I could add her... No, wait, their handles are probably different...*

Would she even show up? I waited and waited, taking tiny sips of ginger ale. In front of me on the table was a second, empty glass. I had told the front desk clerk that I was expecting someone to meet me here, so it would be extra humiliating if she didn't come. Doubly so after all the other times we came here together. It would probably look like I got dumped.

Actually, now that I thought about it—while it must have taken a *tremendous* amount of courage for a girl to invite a guy into a private room, didn't the opposite give kind of...creeper vibes...?

Just then, the knob on the soundproof door rattled loudly as it turned, and...

"Hi there, Takigawa-san," I greeted her.

"What do you want from me?"

Her voice was as cold as her glare. This was the Takigawa Kazune of my world, exactly as I always imagined her to be...but after spending all that time with Kazune, it seemed so strange and out of character.

"Look, just have a seat, okay? Oh, and the drinks are free. Want me to get you something?"

"No, I'm fine right here, thank you."

She continued to stand at the entrance to the room, hand on the knob, suggesting she didn't trust me as far as she could throw me. Did she have a bad time with parallel Koyomi? Surely they must have talked to each other at some point, right? Either way, there was no point in dragging this out, so I got straight to it.

"You recently spent a week in World 85, right?"

Her answer was hesitant. "Yes."

"Did you talk to my parallel self there?"

"Yes."

"Cool."

So far, so good. So what was my next move? *"What was I like?"* Zero chance she wouldn't think it was a stupid question. Man, who would have thought a friendless loser like me would ever casually strike up a conversation with Takigawa-san? This, too, I owed entirely to Kazune. As I was lost in thought, low-key hoping to flee from my awkward reality, the unthinkable happened. Takigawa-san started to say something to me.

"Um..." she said.

"Hm?"

"Did you...talk to *her* too? My...parallel self?" she stammered, averting her gaze. Evidently, she was just as curious as I was. Not that I blamed her at all. Maybe Koyomi told her about Kazune's personality and she had the same reaction I did.

"Yeah, we came here every day after school. Talked about all sorts of stuff."

"Like what?" Takigawa-san asked.

"Oh, you know. Parallel worlds, imaginary science... We sang some karaoke too. What else... Oh yeah, Kazune told me her relationship with Koyomi wasn't going well."

"Kazune?"

"Oh, uh...s-sorry. She told me to call her that because 'the version of you from your world' was too much of a mouthful. If it makes you uncomfortable, I'll stop."

"...No, it's fine." With a small sigh, she finally relented and sat down across from me at the table. She left the door ajar, however. "So...er... What was she like?"

"What?"

"You know... Kazune..."

She still refused to meet my gaze, but I suspected she was on the same page as me. I figured I'd answer her question before I asked her about Koyomi.

"Well, to put it simply... Gosh, how do I describe her..." I thought back to her face, her voice, her word choice. We only had a single week together, an hour per day max, and yet it felt like a truly special memory.

Probably because I'm in—

"She was really smart, and surprisingly friendly, and some-times a total bully... Oh, and she was in love," I said.

"Love..." With that, Takigawa-san hung her head even lower.

What was concealed beneath that curtain of hair—behind those glasses? What was on her mind? At this point, I felt a far stronger connection to Kazune 85 than I did to the version of her that actually belonged here.

"Hey, uh..." I decided to come right out and say it. "Look, it has nothing to do with the relationship we have in that parallel world, but..."

My heart was pounding so hard it threatened to burst out of my ribcage. The way I felt writing that note to her was *nothing* compared to this. But I had to say it. It was the entire reason I invited her here. She stared down wordlessly at the floor, waiting for me to continue, but I was struggling to find the courage to finish. Maybe I'd never be like Koyomi.

Then I remembered what Kazune had said to me previously. *"If you're angling for that, you'll have to give it your best."*

Yeah, that's it... Come on, me! I gotta give it my best shot!

And so, I forced the words out. "Would, uh... W-would you wanna...be friends with me?"

Oh god.

Oh god, I said it.

My entire body broke out into a sweat and my face burned hot. It was way too early to say I was in love with her, much less ask her to be my girlfriend. That was why I wanted to start as friends first...but who would have thought it would be just as nerve-racking?

And what was her reaction? I snuck a peek at her, but she was still hanging her head, so I couldn't see her expression.

"Friends...?" she muttered, without looking up.

Was it too much to ask, to be friends with a guy like me? Kazune had suggested we might be destined for each other, but clearly she was wrong. The anxiety was killing me. Feeling like I might burst into tears, I stared at her as she sat there in silence.

"...Kh..."

Her head and shoulders began to tremble... And then...

"Kkhh...keh heh...ha ha! Ha ha ha ha ha!!! I can't keep a straight face...!" Takigawa-san burst out laughing. "T-Takasaki-kun! 'Friends'? *That's* what you wanted to ask?!"

"Wh-what...?!" I couldn't understand what was going on. Even Kazune had never laughed so uncontrollably in front of me! Was she always like this? "T-Takigawa-san...?"

"Hee hee hee! Look!" Still giggling, she showed me the IP band on her wrist.

The LCD screen showed...085.

"...What?! K-Kazune?!"

Takigawa-san—no, *Kazune*!—saw the shock on my face and burst out laughing all over again. Three days ago, she led me to think she shifted back home, but it was all just an act!

"How could you trick me like that?! I thought you finally went back home! I was happy for you, damn it!" If only she knew how sad I was when I realized I never got to say goodbye to her! ...Not that I'd say that out loud and embarrass myself further!

"Okay, seriously though... Why did you wait so long? Did you honestly agonize for three days straight...over asking me to be *friends* with you?" she asked, incredulous.

Yes!!!

"Ha ha... *Ha ha ha!* My sides...my sides are in orbit...!"

With one arm wrapped around her waist, she grabbed my glass off the table and downed what remained of my ginger ale. Normally I might've been thrilled at the thought of this indirect kiss, but my brain didn't have room to consider that right now. I snatched my glass back from her, tilted it back, and crunched the ice between my molars. It cooled my face ever so slightly. My head was a mess, but I needed to try (however unsuccessfully) to keep her from finding out, so I donned my best poker face.

"So you still haven't shifted back? Now I'm *really* concerned," I said.

"Oh, uh... Here, Takasaki-kun, take a look."

She showed me her IP band again—was she that tickled to have tricked me?

"Yes, I get it, thanks! The gullible idiot totally fell for it! Happy?"

"Not that!" Still guffawing away, she reached over to her band's LCD screen...and peeled off the "085" with her fingers. "It was just a sticker. Looked real, though, didn't it?"

"...What?!"

Beneath the sticker, on the real LCD screen, was the number 000.

My mind went blank. I couldn't understand. Logically, the answer was simple, but my brain didn't even try to process it.

"When we first spoke here, you asked me why I didn't think to check my IP band. Do you remember what I said in response?"

"That...you were used to shifting one or two worlds away all the time and barely noticed a difference. So you stopped bothering." As far as I could recall, that was more or less what she said to me at the time.

"These prototypes are loaned out for *testing purposes*. Everyone who wears one is required to check and report their IP number on a daily basis. I'd never forget to do that!"

"So...what are you saying?"

"What I'm *saying*..." she said as she donned the biggest smirk I'd ever seen. She then revealed the truth. "I never parallel shifted to begin with. 'Kazune from World 85' doesn't exist—I was the Takigawa Kazune from World Zero the entire time."

Right. It was just that simple. The day she called me Koyomi, when she looked at her IP band and got flustered, when she told me she and I were lovers in another world, and that it was going poorly... All of it was a lie. A performance.

What I didn't understand was...

"Why would you do that?" I asked, choking the words out as best I could manage. I was too confused to be angry. If Kazune was the Takigawa-san from my world the whole time, then that was the first time either of us had ever spoken to each other. Why would she do this to a total stranger?

At my question, the smile faded from her face. She answered with a single word.

"Revenge."

"What?"

"You tricked me, so I wanted to trick you back," she said.

"...I have no clue what you're talking about."

I swear, I couldn't think of a single possible thing. Sure, I was a loser, but I was *positive* I never deceived anyone in my life. As such, the very next words she said took me a moment to process.

"Valedictorian," she said simply.

"Huh?"

"You declined it, didn't you?"

"What? How did you—" I started.

"Prior to the entrance ceremony, when I got that call from the school asking me to speak as the class valedictorian, I was beyond ecstatic. I even bragged to my parents that I got the highest score on the entrance exam to the prefecture's most competitive high school! They were so proud of me! And I was proud to give that speech!"

Ah. At last, I was starting to understand.

"Then, after the ceremony, I accidentally overheard the teachers in the staff room talking about how relieved they were that I agreed to the role after the *real* highest scorer declined. I stormed in there and demanded to know who it was. Only then did I learn the truth so unjustly hidden from me!"

Right. So that was what she meant.

"Do you have *any idea* how bitter and pathetic I felt? From that moment on, I vowed I would outscore you on every test. But then, for whatever reason, you started getting bad grades on purpose!"

"How did you know?" I asked.

"Are you kidding? 97, 89, 83, 79, 73—they're all *prime numbers.* It was so obvious!"

"I'll think of a new pattern from now on."

"My point is, you never gave me an opportunity to *really* compete with you. That's why I decided I'd pull one over on you and have a hearty laugh at your expense!"

"...You're a real odd duck, you know that?"

"Yes, I get that a lot."

Frankly, it all made sense. She thought she earned that title through her own academic prowess, but then she found out it was a hand-me-down from me. She then tried to retroactively "earn" it by beating me on another exam—but I was screwing around the whole time, collecting prime numbers. Yep, I was partly to blame for this.

Still... To think that she'd plot out this wild prank and spend a full ten days fooling me... And with the kind of acting performance that could win awards...

There was no doubt about it. I was in love with—

"Kazune?"

"What is it?"

"Would you maybe... I mean, will you be my girlfriend?"

She chuckled. "No."

Then, after a pause...

"The Koyomi *I* love is a manly man who would charge in to rescue me from a weirdo. So no, I can't date you, Takasaki-kun."

• • •

And there you have it. My first-ever romantic confession ended in a spectacular failure. That was how I, Takasaki Koyomi, met Takigawa Kazune—my beloved wife.

To Every You
I've Loved Before

Interlude

AFTER I MET KAZUNE, my life slowly started to change. First of all, I began taking tests seriously again—*all* of them, even the pop quizzes. Kazune had been continually holding the top spot in our class, but I immediately dethroned her. Sometimes we tied at 100 points, but not once in my high school career did I let her outscore me after that.

She was the type of person who wanted to win by any means necessary, and believe it or not, she started asking me to tutor her. As soon as class ended, she'd come to me with questions, and whenever a teacher handed back a graded test, I'd have to spend my whole lunch break reviewing it with her. In exchange, I lost all my reading time, but I was catastrophically terrible at explaining things, so I needed the practice.

And besides, deep down, part of me was just happy Kazune and I were still talking. I was still in love with her, even though she turned me down.

But *that* was where things got interesting. Now that Kazune and I were holding study sessions between classes, our classmates naturally saw this as the school's two highest academic performers working together to better themselves. It wasn't long until their fragile intellectualist egos compelled them to ask to join us. Then, as our study group gradually expanded and the grade average of Class A shot through the roof, the last few stubborn holdouts in the class finally caved. The group got bigger, and our class's grade average improved even more.

I say our class was "intellectualist," but to be fair, we were all just teenagers. There was something magical about working on a project together, and before I knew it, the vibe of the class had completely relaxed. Soon we were going out to karaoke together, just like Kazune's imagined "World 85," and the number of people I counted as friends began to grow.

After that, well...we were teenagers! The topics of discussion were bound to shift away from schoolwork, eventually. Sure enough, some started to talk about pop culture and romance, and before long, someone finally asked the question. *"What exactly is going on between you and Takigawa-san?"*

At school, Kazune maintained her quiet, aloof "Takigawa-san" persona. She was always cautiously polite, even with peers, and she didn't fraternize more than strictly necessary. But with me, she was a bit more relaxed. She was also the only person in class I referred to by their first name. It was only natural that people would suspect something.

Unfortunately, I didn't know how to respond to that.

I couldn't exactly tell them about her big revenge plot... Well, to be totally honest, I didn't *want* to tell them. I wanted it to stay a special memory that only she and I knew about. My only option was to admit that I asked her out and she turned me down. They were shocked to hear it.

Over the next two years and until my high school graduation, I would enlist the support of basically my entire first-year class (minus a few who ended up in separate programs) to re-confess my feelings for Kazune a total of five different times. They all ended in rejection. I was really hoping she'd go for it the fifth time, on graduation day even, but alas, all I got was a smile and her usual curt "no."

And with that, Kazune and I went off to college.

• • •

Kyushu University Faculty of Science, Department of Imaginary Science. The first university in the world to offer a formal degree in imaginary science.

The Kyushu region was generally considered to be at the forefront of imaginary science innovation. In fact, the woman who originally discovered and established the field, Satou Itoko, was a physics student at Kyushu U. From there, she transferred to a graduate school in Germany before coming back to Japan to become the country's youngest professor. She then established the Imaginary Science Research Institute (ISRI) and set about proving her theory. My dad and Kazune's dad were both friends with her in college, and they all went on to work at the ISRI together.

Their efforts would pay off approximately ten years later, right around the time I was ten years old. It was then that Professor Satou went back to Germany and announced she had proven the existence of parallel worlds at a scientific conference—sparking unprecedented levels of debate as scientific organizations across the globe came together to try to verify (or debunk) this lofty claim. And just three short years later, each and every international scientific authority confirmed the ISRI's findings. Imaginary science was now an accepted field of study.

The following year, Kyushu University added a Department of Imaginary Science to its Faculty of Science. A handful of researchers that included Professor Satou were invited to teach there part-time, offering lessons on the latest discoveries in the field. In order to study imaginary science, Kazune and I both enrolled there. Our high school was all too eager to give us their letters of recommendation, and after we survived the interview stage, we left our hometown of Oita City, and both got our own apartments in Fukuoka.

Seeing as we were both moving to the same place, I thought I may as well ask her to live with me (love confession #6), but she turned me down again, explaining she wanted to see what it was like to live on her own. I was perhaps the only guy in the world who had been rejected by the same woman six separate times. However, at this point, I was starting to lean into it. I decided I'd keep asking her out until the day she found someone else.

But then, during the summer of our first year at college, she randomly showed up at my apartment one weekend and dropped a bombshell on me.

"Oh, that reminds me, Takasaki-kun. I had a favor I wanted to ask."

"Hm? What's up?" I figured she might need to borrow some money, but I couldn't remember offhand how much I had in my wallet.

"Could you go out with me?"

All right, deep breaths now... We're not gonna fall for it. She doesn't mean it like that. She probably has an errand to run or something.

"Sure thing. Need an extra pair of hands to carry your shopping bags?" This statement was approximately 90 percent serious and 10 percent hoping to be wrong.

"No, that's not what I meant. Could you be my boyfriend?"

All right, deep breaths now... We're not gonna fall for it. She doesn't mean it like that. She... She means the other *kind of boyfriend... You know, uhhh... Wait, what the hell is she talking about?!*

I was extremely confused. Who was she, and what had she done with my Kazune? Was she pranking me again? Instead of saying yes and jumping for joy, I just sat there and frowned suspiciously.

"Why?" I asked.

This was close to the worst possible response to a woman confessing her feelings. But could you blame me?

That being said, her answer was even harsher than mine.

"I've been getting a lot more male attention now that we're in college. It's annoying. I thought I should find myself a boyfriend and put an end to it, and... Eh, you'll do."

Or something to that effect. Can you imagine how I felt hearing that? The joy of her finally accepting my love, but also the fury of how she chose to phrase it. If only I could go back in time and see the look on my face...

Point being, I didn't give her an answer right away. In fact, I even considered saying no. It'd be a hilarious plot twist after all that. But when I saw her sitting there, staring at the floor and avoiding my gaze with her noticeably red ears peeking through her hair... It was so unbearably adorable that I ended up letting it all slide.

And that was how I went from Takasaki-kun to Koyomi.

• • •

I lived a mostly fulfilling college life, interspersed with time spent with Kazune. After four straight years of excellent grades, both Kazune and I were encouraged to consider grad school, but neither of us cared about getting a Master's or a PhD. Instead of spending another two to five years studying and networking, we wanted to get into the field and start actually *researching*. As a result, after we graduated college—as class valedictorian and salutatorian, of course—we went home to Oita, where our passion and skill was rewarded with employment at the ISRI.

Meanwhile, society was starting to see parallel shifting as a normal part of life. The world was on the cusp of widespread IP band implementation, and tester versions had been made available to the public. I began wearing one myself back when I started college, and it was finally starting to sink in just how commonplace minor parallel shifts truly were. Whenever I couldn't find something in its "usual" place, I'd check my IP band and, sure enough, I'd find that I was one to three worlds away from home.

Of course, there were still plenty of people who refused to accept the concept as anything more than fiction, but society was quickly leaving those people behind. As for the rest of us—those who had chosen to accept, or *try* to accept, the coming revolution—we were slowly but steadily transitioning to a brand-new world.

Now, then...this naturally led all of humanity to a single, major question.

Were our parallel selves still *us*?

To Every You
I've Loved Before

CHAPTER 3

Adulthood

TODAY, IT'S WIDELY ACCEPTED that an engagement ring should cost approximately three months' salary. Supposedly, this was first cooked up by some jewelry store in the 1970s in order to sell rings at a premium. Back then, the average monthly salary was around 100,000 yen, and therefore an engagement ring was worth 300,000 yen. However, because the average salary has gone up quite a lot here in modern times, three months' worth turns out to be a huge chunk of change. That said, the value of gems hasn't gone up much at all, so when buying an engagement ring, they say you should still aim to spend around 300,000 yen regardless of your salary.

Maybe if I was a high earner, I would have splurged on something more expensive, but unfortunately, researchers weren't that well paid. While I had gotten a few raises over three years of hard work, I couldn't afford to go overboard. Therefore, my plan was to buy something at the baseline of 300,000 yen.

I had a strong dislike of credit cards, so I withdrew 500,000 yen in cash (just in case), put it in my wallet, and went into a jewelry store for the first time in my life.

The display cases glittered with dazzling jewels. Beautiful, yes, but when I thought about how many thousands of yen they were going to ask me to pay, I felt the urge to turn around and leave. This wasn't about what *I* wanted, however.

"Looking for something specific?"

A chipper saleswoman about my age walked over to me with a bright smile. Generally, I didn't enjoy it when employees asked me about what I was buying, but when it came to engagement rings, I was clueless. I decided to see what she was like before asking her to help me choose.

"Yeah, uh, an engagement ring."

"Wow, congratulations! How old is she?"

"Uhh, twenty-five?"

"And how long have you been together?"

"Oh, it's been...seven years now, I think."

"Seven years! Awww! That's such a long time... Your girl-friend's a lucky lady. I wish *I* was getting an engagement ring."

Her reaction was surprisingly sweet and bashful, so I decided to trust her judgment. Was I too easily bought? Maybe this was all a script from some customer service manual. Still, it made me feel good, and that was enough for me. "I, uh... I honestly have no clue how I'm supposed to choose."

"Well, there are three types of engagement rings: ready-made, custom-made, and semi-custom. Ready-made rings are the most affordable, and you can have them right away. Semi-custom rings have a few different designs or gems you can choose from in a mix-and-match style, and they take about a month to be finished. Lastly, custom-made rings are unique, one-of-a-kind creations made exactly to your specifications. They take anywhere from two to three months before they're ready, and they're the most expensive."

I didn't know custom orders took that long. Granted, I wasn't in any big hurry to propose to her, but...could I really keep this secret for months on end? I wasn't sure my heart could take it. Honestly, before I came in here, I wasn't even aware custom orders were an option.

"Do most people customize their engagement rings?"

"Nope! When it comes to engagement rings, I'd say...hm, about half of them end up choosing a ready-made style."

"Oh, okay. Then maybe that's what I'll go with. I'd like to have it right away."

"Great! Now, pardon my asking—what's your budget?" the woman asked.

"Somewhere around 300K, but I can go a little over."

"Got it! So, when's her birthday?"

"Uhh... March 25th."

"March, huh? Aquamarine!"

"What?"

"Many customers choose a diamond for their engagement ring, but some opt for birthstones instead," she explained. "If she's born in March, her birthstone is aquamarine, and those are... right over here!"

The gems she pointed to were...teal (I think?) in color—bright, pale blue, like the Okinawan Sea. It was the perfect color to match Kazune's personality.

"Each gemstone has a number of symbolic meanings. For instance, diamonds signify purity, sincerity, joy...and, of course, 'the promise of love' and 'an eternal bond.' That's one reason they're so often chosen for engagement rings."

"I see... So what about aquamarines?"

"Aquamarine represents courage, cunning, and composure. Other meanings include 'a happy marriage' and 'a loving couple.' It's a great choice."

Great? It sounded *perfect*! Courage, cunning, and composure—I couldn't think of a more fitting description of Kazune. I was now completely on board with aquamarine. "Okay then, I think I'd like one of those."

"Wonderful! I'll go get the catalog, so have a seat right there and I'll be back shortly. If the one you like isn't available in our store, we can arrange to have one sent here for you."

As I watched her stroll away, I stiffly sat down in the chair and let out a deep sigh. I was exhausted, and I hadn't even bought the damn thing yet. Also, I noticed her eyes were sparkling the whole time she was talking to me about gemstones... Did all women get that excited about jewelry, even when it wasn't for them? Even Kazune?

Looking back, I hadn't really seen her wear much jewelry over the years. She didn't even have her ears pierced. If anything, she mostly stuck to some clips in her hair. If that was the case...would she even *want* this ring? Would she accept it? The thought of giving it to her made me so nervous I could scarcely breathe.

And...what the hell was I going to say when I proposed to her?

• • •

A few days after I picked up the ring from the jewelry store, I summoned all my courage and asked Kazune to meet me somewhere. The location? Our usual karaoke lounge. Most people would probably think it was a bad place to propose, but for me, it *had* to happen here. This was the very spot where I fell in love with her, after all.

I had a ginger ale, and she had an iced tea—coincidentally the very same drinks we got when we met here the first time. As she fiddled with the karaoke machine to decide on her first song, I set the ring box on the table in front of her, opened the lid, and— with no lead-up whatsoever—said, "Let's get married."

It was the most I could manage. Prior to that moment, I concocted a whole plan—I'd sing some song that was popular back in high school, then casually start reminiscing about old times, say some things about how we stayed together despite it all, and then I'd ask her to be with me for the rest of my life. But despite all my mental run-throughs, the moment she was actually in front of me, that ring started burning a hole in my pocket. My mind went blank, and I skipped all my steps. Before I knew it, I popped the question.

Kazune's eyes widened, and her jaw dropped—a silly expression she rarely ever made normally. Every other time I prepared a surprise for her (like birthdays and such), she always saw through it and laughed in my face. And yet, just this once, it seemed like I actually caught her off-guard. But while I'd always dreamed of getting this reaction out of her, I didn't have the composure to savor it.

She looked at me; I gazed intently back at her. This was no laughing matter, and I didn't dare break eye contact. I stared at her with all the love I could muster.

She then looked down and picked up the tiny box. Her eyes lingered on the ring, sitting there with a pale blue gem adorning it.

"Is this an aquamarine?" she asked quietly.

"Yeah."

Kazune had never seemed all that passionate about jewelry to me, but considering she could identify the gemstone on sight, perhaps she was more interested than I thought. Judging from the look in her eyes, she was practically swooning—though not *solely* over the pretty bauble, I hoped.

Wordlessly, she kept staring down at the piece. Personally, I was in no hurry to get an answer out of her. After all these years and everything we'd been through together, I was confident she wouldn't say no. Still, total silence was a far cry from being reassuring.

Then, out of nowhere, she pointed the open box in my direction. "Um... Will you put it on my finger?"

"...Sure." I took the box from her and pulled the ring out. Then I took her left hand and raised the ring to her ring finger.

I could feel her hand trembling in mine. When I snuck a glance at her, her expression was unreadable, but her ears were bright red. *Classic Kazune.* When she lied about us being lovers in another world, and when she asked me to be her boyfriend, and even when we had our first kiss—she kept a perfect poker face while blushing all the way to her ears.

Meanwhile, the engagement ring slid neatly onto her finger.

"It's a perfect fit... When did I ever tell you my size?"

"I measured you in secret while you were asleep."

I could remember how my heart raced, slooowly trying to wrap a thread around her ring finger as she lay there snoring, all the while praying I wouldn't wake her. But if I hadn't, I never could have gotten her this ring otherwise.

She lovingly stroked the aquamarine in the ring as it sat perfectly perched on her finger. Arguably, I already knew the answer, but I still wanted to hear her say it.

"Kazune?"

"Yes." She nodded gleefully...then bowed her head. "'Til death do us part."

• • •

Our parents had long since known about our relationship, so when we told them we were getting married, their only reaction was "Finally!" However, because both of our families were relatively wealthy, they nearly strong-armed us into having a big, lavish wedding. But neither of us were all that fond of the spotlight, so we desperately convinced them into letting us plan a small ceremony with family only. In exchange, we agreed to hold it on a traditionally auspicious day, lest we jinx anything.

From there, once we reserved a venue, all that remained was to wait six months until the big day. Around the time we were ironing out the small details, however, we encountered a problem—or should I say, *re-encountered*. One that all of humanity was forced to confront sooner or later, now that parallel worlds were an accepted part of life.

I first became strongly aware of this issue during my second year of college. Kazune had just turned twenty, and we decided to celebrate by drinking together for the first time. The party was held at my apartment, just the two of us.

"Happy birthday, Kazune."

"Thank you."

She blew out the candles adorning her mini birthday cake, and the room went dark. Then I got up, flipped the lights on, and opened a bottle of slightly pricey champagne. The pop of the cork and fizz of the bubbles felt like tiny fireworks in my ears.

Together, we ate some cake and each other's home cooking, and then we had our official "first tastes" of alcohol. Both of us lived alone, and with our phones turned off, no one could interrupt our fun. We had yet to consummate the relationship, but she had agreed to spend the night, and we were getting tipsy... I'm not sure if I should say I was *expecting* it, but I was certainly *intending* for us to finally go all the way that night, and I suspected her intention was the same. She drank a tiny bit of alcohol, pretended to get really drunk, then let me guide her to bed, blushing all the way to her ears.

It was the first time for both of us, so we started by awkwardly linking our fingers together. Desperately willing myself to go slow, I peppered kisses across her cheek and neck before starting to take her clothes off.

And then, while I was kissing her left palm, I saw it. Her IP band displayed 001.

Kazune had parallel shifted. The girl I was kissing was the Kazune from the world next door. The instant I processed this, my mind went blank, completely wiping away the pleasant buzz of alcohol and arousal. That was the moment I first became aware of this issue.

There were limitless parallel worlds, and we subconsciously shifted across them on a daily basis. The farther the world, the harder it was to shift there; conversely, worlds within a range of three were nearly identical to our home world, so we'd often shift there and back without ever realizing.

At some point tonight, Kazune had shifted one world over. The closer the world, the smaller the difference, so I suspected our parallel selves had thrown the exact same birthday party we did. But...did that give me the right to have sex with *this* Kazune? Was this really still *my* girlfriend?

"What's wrong?"

She noticed that I stopped and cupped my cheek. Wordlessly, I pointed to her IP band, and she gasped. Now she understood that she was in the world next door.

"What about yours?"

At her prompting, I showed her my IP band: 000. I hadn't shifted.

"I see... Well, this certainly is a pickle," she said.

Like me, she froze for a long moment. Then, with a sigh, she sat up in bed, having returned to her usual self. Frankly, I was in no mood to continue either. I sat beside her and heaved a sigh of my own.

"Should I assume these were very similar circumstances?"

"Probably. We were having drinks for my twentieth birthday, and one thing led to another. No clue when exactly I shifted... As far as I can tell, your room is identical to his."

"Why did it have to be *now*, of all times...?" I complained.

"I'll apologize if you'd like, but it's not really my fault."

"Yeah, I know. Eh, I'm sure there'll be a next time... Back to the booze?"

"Yes, please," she said.

We returned to the dining table and picked up where we left off drinking. I was warned the first time didn't always work out, so I was somewhat prepared for that, but I never thought *this* would be why. Unable to truly escape sobriety, we fumbled our way through conversation until we arrived at our old standby: parallel worlds.

"To think that a mere ten years ago, parallel worlds were purely the stuff of fiction," she said.

"They were researching it well before that, but that's when it first went public, yeah."

"Does that mean people in the past had experiences like these all the time, but simply never noticed? They made love to their parallel partners?"

"They must've. Without our IP bands, I wouldn't have noticed either..." I said. "Man, if we took them off even a moment earlier, we might have kept going without a clue."

"That's a little frightening."

"Yeah... But I mean, to be fair, our worlds are next-door neighbors. We're more or less the same exact people."

"You consider your parallel selves to be the same as you?" she asked.

"For the most part, sure... Oh, but if he was from World 100 or 200 or something, he might be some kind of serial killer. Wouldn't want to associate myself with *that* guy."

"But he's from a parallel world, just like all the rest. Where do you draw the line?"

"Well...*logically*, there probably isn't a line at all," I reasoned.

"So no matter how different they are, they're all still you?"

"Logically, yeah."

"Then...why won't you have sex with me?" she asked.

Why? The answer was simple. "Because I can't think 'logically' when it comes to you. Back in your world, my Kazune is having the same conversation with your Koyomi. I bet they feel almost the exact same way, and they're saying nearly the exact same things. But if I imagined your Koyomi making love to my Kazune? I'd go insane with jealousy."

I didn't want to even *think* about her sleeping with someone else, even if that "someone else" was a parallel version of me. And if I had sex with this Kazune, the same event would probably happen in the other world too. Because of that, I could progress no further.

"Ah. Yes, I can imagine that." Frowning, she took a sip of her drink. She must have envisioned the same thing. Incidentally, because of her low alcohol tolerance, after just one glass of champagne, she had downgraded to a wine cooler with 3% ABV. "But I mean, we've seen so many films about parallel worlds..."

A rather sudden change of topic—or was it? Regardless, I nodded.

In the decade or so before we were born, parallel worlds were a popular theme in manga, books, movies, and TV shows. The woman who founded the real-life Imaginary Science Research Institute, Professor Satou, openly attributed much of her inspiration to those stories, and many of her discoveries and theories were named after them. We consumed a lot of that media ourselves in the name of research as well.

"In almost all of them, the protagonist tries over and over again to change the future into what they want, right? It makes me think—just because the *protagonist* doesn't like what happens in a parallel world, does that make it *bad*? Even though it was constructed by their parallel self?" she asked me.

"Well, people depicted parallel worlds in a lot of different ways back then. But now that we know they're real, those types of stories probably won't get made anymore."

"Right. I mean, time travel isn't even possible. If you really wanted to undo a mistake, I guess you'd have to travel to a distant world where it didn't even happen."

"But then you'd be forcing your failure on a version of you that didn't deserve it," I said.

"If our research continues to develop, I imagine we'll reach that point eventually."

"That's why we need legislation. Even now, our superiors are campaigning for it."

"I know what you mean. After all, who would be at fault if I, say, committed a crime in this world and went home afterwards?" she asked.

"Between neighboring worlds, most likely both of your selves would commit the same crime, anyway. But when it comes to 10 or 20 worlds apart, it's not so clear-cut. And if it's 100 or 200 worlds apart, the victim could be framed for the murder of someone they don't even recognize."

"I really doubt anyone's shifting 100 worlds away completely by chance... Ack!"

Just as our tangents were spiraling out of control, like always, Kazune reached for her wine cooler without looking and accidentally knocked it over onto the floor.

"Oh, I'm so sorry!"

"Nah, it's fine." Grinning, I mopped up the mess with a tissue.

As I did, she cocked her head in confusion. "Wait, did I really put it there...?" Then she looked at her IP band. "Oh!"

"What's up?"

Wordlessly, she showed me the LCD screen: 000.

"Oh, hey, welcome back," I said.

"Thank you. Goodness, the transition really is seamless."

I hadn't noticed anything visually different about her or heard any hiccups in the conversation, so I truly had no clue when they switched back. She must have set her drink down in a slightly different location in the other world, and since she didn't notice anything amiss, she must have been having the *exact* same discussion over there. Close-range parallel shifts caused little accidents like this all the time.

After I finished cleaning the floor, we looked back at each other.

"Well, I'm home now, so shall we...continue?" she asked sheepishly.

"No, I'm not really in the mood anymore."

Laughing at ourselves, we let our first time end in failure. Ultimately, we made up for it less than a month later—though we kept our IP bands on and checked periodically, just in case. It was something of a stressful experience all around.

In summary, this was a major question brought about by the progress of imaginary science: were our parallel selves still us?

Thus far, the world had yet to find an answer.

• • •

We next revisited this question approximately two months before our wedding was set to be held. As I held Kazune in my arms, she sleepily asked, "Hey, Koyomi? Do you think we'll really be able to get married?"

"Why do you say that?"

"Well, what if one of us parallel shifts on the big day?" she asked me. "Are we supposed to simply get married to that parallel self? Or should we stop the ceremony?"

This was probably her way of expressing pre-wedding jitters. I'd wondered the same thing myself, but I decided there was no point in thinking about it. Instead, I chose unfounded optimism. *Whatever happens, happens.* Looking back, however, it strikes me as a weird position for me to take. Maybe I was afraid to think about it too hard.

Now that Kazune was starting to agonize over it, however, I could feel the anxiety creeping back in. What was I going to do if something like that *did* happen? After failing to find an answer on my own, I suddenly remembered my father's research.

At the ISRI where Kazune and I worked, each department was staffed by a small team with their own research objectives. My father's team was focused on what we called IP stabilization.

Imaginary science was founded upon the concept of *imaginary space*, or an infinite probability space filled with imaginary elements. Variation in these elements gave shape to physical particles, and the differences caused by those variations were said to give form to parallel worlds. The pattern created by each world's variable particles was called the Imaginary Elements Print, or IP for short.

Accordingly, the function of an IP band was to measure the differences between two IPs and quantify them in numerical form. However, they didn't *actually* measure imaginary elements themselves, but rather the physical particles manifested by those imaginary elements. This was our workaround until we found a way to observe an imaginary space directly.

As for IP stabilization, it involved observing imaginary elements overlaid in an imaginary space, then freezing the quantum state and preventing any flux. Were we to achieve this, we would then be able to prevent parallel shifts, or so the theory went. The problem was, how could human beings *measure* imaginary elements when we couldn't *observe* them? That was the key to my father's research.

If we could achieve IP stabilization, then Kazune and I could "lock" our IPs for the day of the wedding to prevent any parallel shifts. That sort of thing was partly why the ISRI was researching it to begin with—that, and to prevent future parallel criminals from shifting away from their punishments.

Though we all worked at the same lab, ISRI teams were generally expected to keep their progress under wraps until they had achieved a certain degree of success. My father had accidentally leaked this information to me during a private conversation. He made me promise not to tell anyone, so I hadn't said anything to Kazune yet, but...surely I was allowed to talk to *him* about it, right? Therefore, I went with him to the deserted lab over the weekend to ask him for advice regarding the wedding. He told me that his team hadn't achieved IP stabilization yet, but even if they had, there were so many unknown variables and risks that it would likely be quite a while before they could test it on people.

"Koyomi..." he started. "I'm starting to think I should stop researching this."

"What?! How come?" I couldn't believe my ears. My father was practically *married* to his research! Could IP stabilization really be that challenging?

"First, what do you think a parallel world is?" he asked me.

"Um... A separate world that branches off from past events?"

"Right. In other words, a manifestation of possibility."

"I beg your pardon?"

"Say your breakfast options this morning were onigiri or toast. If you picked onigiri, then the *possibility* of you picking toast is itself a parallel world. Each and every world in existence represents a choice we never made."

I imagined two selves: one who ate onigiri and one who ate toast, each of them living in their own separate world.

"Now, let's think about what IP stabilization really means. When it comes down to it, I fear it's a lot like if we took away the toast and *forced* you to choose the other," he said.

Ah. Admittedly, that sounded like a bad deal. After all, having the ability to choose was part of what made life so great.

"Choosing onigiri after some thought or having no other option. The outcome may seem the same, but the first case manifests two selves: one who ate onigiri and one who ate toast. In the second, there can only *be* the self who ate onigiri... You see?"

His analogy was easy to understand, but I found myself circling back to the start. It felt like we were taking breakfast *way* too seriously. Regardless, I gave my best answer.

"Okay, so parallel worlds represent possibilities, and IP stabilization *erases* those possibilities and makes it so no new parallel worlds are born. Right?"

"That's right. The self who wants onigiri ends up killing off the self who wanted toast, all for his own gain. That's what I fear IP stabilization is... I just can't shake it."

"Look, Dad, I get what you're saying, but..."

This wasn't about breakfast foods. This was about my wedding—a once-in-a-lifetime event. Even supposing he was right, in this particular case, the only possibility getting erased was the possibility of Kazune and me not getting married! Of *course* I wanted it gone!

When I explained this to him, he fell into thought for a long moment.

Eventually, he said to me, "When I married your mother, we didn't *have* IP bands."

No kidding. Back then, imaginary science possibly didn't even exist yet. Those were the days when parallel worlds were still the stuff of fiction.

He then continued. "It's possible the woman I married was actually a parallel self. But even if it was, I have no regrets—because I truly loved her."

Love. He said it without a hint of embarrassment, and oddly enough, I found that I wasn't embarrassed either.

"Even though we're not together anymore, I still love her—*every* her in *every* world. I love everything about her, and that includes all her possibilities."

"*All* her possibilities...?"

"That's right. If you can do that, then you don't *need* to lock your IP. Just have the wedding with your head held high."

"I *do* get what you're saying, but..." I realized I was repeating myself and fell silent.

Could I love all of Kazune's possibilities? Including parallel Kazunes from other worlds? If so, then it wouldn't matter if she shifted on our big day. I'd still end up marrying the woman I loved. Putting it simply, Dad was saying our parallel selves were still us.

I could understand his outlook. If I had to guess, I was probably capable of loving every Kazune. She'd shifted dozens of times since we started dating, and all of her parallel selves were still the same woman. The problem for me was the reverse. Could I accept *my* parallel selves loving *my* Kazune? It was an incredibly selfish question to ponder. Put another way, *I* was perfectly okay with cheating on Kazune, but *she* wasn't allowed to do the same, even if the "other man" in this scenario was my parallel self.

My father waited quietly for me to finish thinking it through—but eventually, after the silence dragged on past his limit, he made a suggestion.

"What if you test it out?" he asked.

"What?"

"You know how the director's research team has been working on a way to overwrite IP values in order to cause a controlled parallel shift? Well, their experiments have been successful."

Finally, after all these years! My heart soared with excitement. In high school, when Kazune pretended she shifted here from a distant parallel world, I asked my father if there was any way to shift at will. At the time, he told me it was theoretically possible, but would take another ten years to achieve. Now that those ten years had passed, it was finally approaching the realm of possibility.

"If we can finalize this technology—*optional shifting*—the idea is that we'll be able to send people home when they shift here from distant worlds and vice versa. So far, a handful of experiments using objects and animals have succeeded. At this stage, I'm told all that's left is to run clinical trials."

Now I understood what he was trying to say.

"There are a few obstacles, however. First, we have to apply for authorization from the Institutional Review Board at the Ministry of Health, Labor, and Welfare. That's assuming we can resolve all the ethical and safety concerns...but frankly, a lot of times those concerns *need* clinical trials in order for us to figure out how to resolve them. It's a catch-22. Even if we fudge the numbers in order to get the green light, the board will have regular inspections that interrupt the experiments."

I always heard that clinical trials served as a hurdle in just about any field, not just scientific research. It all came down to how you chose to *overcome* that hurdle.

"Now, I wouldn't go shouting this from the rooftops, but...one strategy that laboratories often utilize is to have fellow researchers serve as subjects in a mock clinical trial."

Basically—secret, possibly illegal human experimentation.

"Of course, they'll take the utmost precautions to make sure you're safe. In accordance with official informed consent standards, patients are given a full explanation of the trial process and the risks involved. Participation is completely optional, *but* if the mock trial can establish proper safety protocols, then it's another step toward official authorization."

In summary, he was suggesting that I take part in the optional shift mock trial.

"You'll start by going to the world next door. It's one you've undoubtedly been to on a daily basis. And since it's right next to us, they'll almost certainly be doing the same test, so the parallel self that arrives in your place will be one that consented to the shift. That saves us needing to explain anything, so the return shift will progress smoothly."

Two selves, consensually switching places. If we could make *that* a reality, there was truly no telling what progress we'd make next!

"Of course, this counts as a facet of your work, so it's your duty as a researcher to take part in the experiment the other world is running too. If all goes well, they'll gradually start sending you out farther and farther. By exchanging information and technology with other worlds, we're hoping not just our field, but *all of humanity* will take a massive leap forward."

The benefits to society were astronomical. The mere thought of it made me dizzy.

"Now, when doing this kind of work, you can expect to have downtime. Not like we do our research 24/7, right?"

"Some days it can feel like it though," I commented.

"...Yeah, sometimes. My point is, if you optional shift to a parallel world, you can use the time you spend there to see if you can love that world's Takigawa-kun. In return, your parallel self will come here and see if he can love *this* world's Takigawa-kun. Why not try and see if you can handle every you loving your lover?"

When I told Kazune about this suggestion, we ultimately decided that both of us would take part in the mock trial. We would find out if we were capable of loving each other's every last possibility, and if we could let those possibilities love us back. And a few days later, we were escorted into a room at the lab that we never had access to before.

In the center of the room was a large capsule designed for one person to lie inside. This, we were told, was the magnetic field generator that would trigger the optional shifts.

"I knew it," I whispered before I could stop myself.

Back when I was a kid, when I parallel shifted to a world where my grandfather was still alive, I woke up in this very pod. Of course, it probably wasn't *literally* the exact same one, but nonetheless, this reunion made me feel strangely emotional.

Director Satou Itoko, founder of the ISRI and imaginary science as a whole, referred to the machine as the "Cradle of Einzwach," but the other researchers just called it the IP capsule. It was common for her to borrow a fanciful name from some dusty old work of fiction, while everyone else went with something more practical.

She explained the trial process to us as follows.

"First, the subject will climb inside the Cradle of Einzwach.

Then, we'll activate the magnetic field generator from outside. The magnetic field will force your body's particles to spin on a different vector, thereby overwriting your IP and shifting you to a world that matches the new IP. That's the basic overview of how it works. If we can resolve the negative effects of magnets on the human body and ensure the subject can return home to World Zero, it'll open the door to authorization for a real clinical trial."

"I notice there's only one capsule...er, Cradle," I commented.

"We can't afford to make a ton of them. Do you have *any idea* how expensive this thing was to construct?"

Whatever figure I was imagining, there were probably a lot more zeroes at the end.

"Now, who wants to go first?"

"I will," I said, immediately raising my hand. Kazune grasped my other hand with a worried frown. I gave her a little squeeze and smiled reassuringly. "It's okay. Hang tight and I'll pave a path for you to follow."

"...Okay."

She nodded without objection. *Who are you and what have you done with my Kazune?! Just kidding.* It was nice not needing to hide our relationship since everyone at the lab already knew about it.

And so Kazune and I took turns shifting. By participating in this mock trial, we were officially added to the research team, and whoever wasn't currently shifting was instead taught how to operate the machine and read the gauges. We both got a little pay raise too—a bonus perk neither of us was expecting.

A few days after orientation, our first-ever shift trial was set to be conducted. These experiments were performed late at night, just to be safe. After all, if we shifted while our other self was driving a car or something, it could cause a major accident. I lay inside the capsule, suppressing my anxiety just enough to smile at Kazune through the glass. She nodded back slightly, then took her position at the console.

"Five, four, three, two, one... Shift: on!"

As the countdown began, I closed my eyes. The magnetic field only took a few seconds to activate, and after that, the shift itself happened in a split-second. Other than a hint of warmth in the air inside the capsule, I didn't feel anything different. Then the glass door opened, and I was greeted by...the exact same people.

"Can you check your IP for me?" the director asked, without pausing to ask how I was feeling.

Nervously, I looked at my band. If the screen displayed 001, the shift was a success...but would it...?

"...001."

"Success! Welcome, Takasaki Koyomi-kun from the world next door."

And so our first-ever optional shift trial was a resounding success. Over the next month or so, Kazune and I traveled between different worlds; when we got there, we were always inside the same IP capsule, which meant all of our selves in all the neighboring worlds had had the same idea. That said, beyond an IP of 004, small differences became more and more apparent, like the position of the furniture in our rooms, or the cars we drove.

In World 7, I had apparently shaved my head, which was refreshingly different from the usual. But what was most valuable to me personally was that I got to see other Kazunes doing these experiments right alongside me.

During my first optional shift, when the two of us had a private moment, we immediately showed each other our IP bands. Mine read 001 and hers was 000. The world next door was nearly identical to mine, so Kazune 1 fully understood what we were doing and why. Thus, the first thing we did was go to our usual karaoke lounge.

"Nice to meet you... No, it's really not the first time, is it?"

"No, I imagine we've met without realizing several times before now—and we've had at least one conversation where we *did* realize."

Yes, I certainly remembered that. Her twentieth birthday—the night our "first time" ended in failure. I could recall seeing 001 on her IP band that night.

"Feels weird, doesn't it? To be totally honest, you don't seem the slightest bit different from Kazune 0," I said.

"In this world, I *am* Kazune 0. But yes, you don't seem any different yourself."

That much was to be expected, of course. The difference between our worlds was as trivial as what we'd eaten for breakfast. And naturally, I recognized the ring on her left ring finger. "Oh hey, it's an aquamarine."

"Yes, er... Well...I suppose I should thank you."

"What brought that on?"

"You gave this ring to your Kazune as well, yes? So I figured I may as well thank you on behalf of all of us."

It was such a bizarre feeling. Everything else was exactly the same, and yet the person in front of me wasn't the same Kazune I proposed to.

"You're still gonna marry me, right?"

"Of course. I mean, I want to. Is that not the whole reason why we joined this trial?"

"Yeah, and it's your turn next, huh? Well, don't sweat it. It's really easy."

"I'm not worried about the trial itself. It's the part that actually matters to us. Finding out whether we can love the others—and allow them to love us in return."

I nodded. Could we love our parallel counterparts? And could we accept those same parallel counterparts loving our beloved?

"To be totally honest... I don't think I'll have trouble with the first part. If you asked me to have sex with you, I'd probably say yes."

"Yes, and perhaps I would. But the problem is..."

"The reverse, yeah. Back in my World Zero, I suspect your Koyomi is having the exact same conversation with my Kazune. The question is, can we accept that?"

"How are you feeling about it right now?"

It was a very difficult question to answer...but... "Personally, I have no intention of sleeping with you tonight."

"Right."

"That means *your* Koyomi most likely doesn't want to sleep with *my* Kazune, so that's a relief. But if I ever *do* make love to a parallel Kazune—all the while knowing my parallel self will make love to *my* Kazune—it'll prove that I've truly accepted it."

"And if you *can't* make love to a parallel me, then...we can't get married?" she asked me.

"Well... I think that's a separate issue..."

"Ugh, this is so obtuse. I kind of wish they'd never discovered parallel worlds at all."

"Yeah, I feel you. Before now, people could live happily, never knowing," I replied.

Surely everyone had felt this way at least once since the advent of parallel worlds. But now that we'd discovered them, we had no choice but to live in a society reshaped by the idea.

Over the following month, the mock trials went reasonably well, with no major incidents. Kazune and I discovered that our relationship was a happy one in pretty much every other world. I still hadn't slept with any parallel Kazunes, but I could feel my mindset slowly shifting.

What *did* bring about tremendous change between me and Kazune, however, was our tenth and final shift experiment.

• • •

When I next awoke, I wasn't inside the IP capsule, but my own bedroom. The lights were off, so I checked the time on my phone. It was just past 2 a.m., the exact time of our shift. However, when I checked my IP band, I felt my stomach drop.

035.

The experiment was supposed to send me to World 10, but suddenly I was all the way in World 35. That was a *huge* leap. Had someone made a mistake with the machine?

In Worlds 1 through 9, I had woken up in the same IP capsule, so I was able to exchange information with my father standing right there. But this world's version of me didn't seem to be taking part in the mock trials at all. If so, then it was possible no one was even at the lab right now. That being the case, I decided I'd wait until morning to head to work.

I spent those few hours in a haze somewhere between sleep and insomnia. Then, when the sun rose, I left my room and walked down the stairs. So far, it was the same house as back home—my grandparents and Yuno had all passed away, so it was just my mother and me living here now. (Kazune was supposed to join us here soon, but given that this was 35 worlds away from mine, I couldn't be sure that still applied.)

"...Morning," I called out timidly to the figure standing in the kitchen.

"Oh, good morning! You're up early. Breakfast isn't ready quite yet."

The familiar sound of my mother's voice instantly put me at ease.

"Mom, we need to talk... My IP is 035 right now."

"*Thirty-five!* You've traveled a long way," she commented.

"Yeah, I gotta go to the lab and ask around about stuff, so I might not come home until late tonight. Don't stay up waiting, okay?"

"Yes, dear. So, World 35, huh? That's incredible, sweetheart! Isn't it supposed to be really rare to shift from that far away?"

"Yeah, it rarely ever happens naturally. But I was taking part in an experiment, so I think that's what caused it."

"Oh dear. Well, promise Mommy you won't do anything too dangerous, okay?"

"It's *fine*, Mom. I'm fine."

Though I was 35 worlds away from home, I could still have a normal conversation with my mother, and she didn't seem put off in the slightest. I expected her to ask a lot more questions about my home world, but since she didn't, I decided not to ask her anything either. Instead, I ate breakfast and headed off to the lab like usual.

The streets were practically identical, as was the location of the ISRI. First thing I did was pay a visit to the research room where my father worked. I wasn't authorized to set foot inside, so instead I asked him to meet me in a common area. Luckily, he wasn't busy, so he showed up right away.

"What's the matter, kiddo?"

"Well, take a look." Without another word, I showed him my IP band.

"*Thirty-five?!* What the hell happened?" he asked me.

I explained to him that we were doing shift experiments back in my world.

"I see... So in *your* world, you signed up for the mock trial. We're doing one in this world too, but with someone else."

Sure enough, my suspicions were right. In that case, there

really must have been some mistake on our end that sent me here. "Will I be able to go home?"

"Yes, of course you can. I'll speak to the director to get permission for you to use the capsule. But since you're here, you should really stay a few days! We don't get many opportunities to exchange information with a world as distant as yours!"

"Oh, okay, sure. I'm fine with that."

"Excellent! Let's get started right away! You wait here and I'll fetch the director!"

He seemed uncharacteristically excited about this, but I understood why. There was nothing quite so alluring as the chance to learn about a distant parallel world. And so after the director came rushing over, we held an emergency meeting—then proceeded to spend the rest of that day exchanging research notes.

• • •

By the time I was finally set free, it was 8 p.m. Now it was time to accomplish my other goal—interacting with parallel Kazune. A long-distance shift was the perfect chance to test if I could truly love *every* her.

It had been hours and I still hadn't glimpsed her yet. Part of me wondered if maybe she had a different job in this world, but when I checked the employee roster, sure enough, she was on it—she was just on a different research team. The system said she was still clocked in though, so I decided to sit in the lounge by the entrance and wait for her.

Approximately twenty minutes later, she arrived at the lobby, bustling along at an unusually fast pace for someone in heels. As she headed for the door, I gave chase and called after her like it was any other day.

"Kazune!"

"Hmm? Oh, Takasaki-kun. How was your day at work?"

It felt so deeply, viscerally *wrong*. She called me *Takasaki-kun*—a term of address my Kazune hadn't used since before we started dating back in our first year of college. Even in World 9, she always called me Koyomi. *If I was "Takasaki-kun" here, then...*

"Did you need something?"

As I tried to think of how to answer, my eyes wandered to her left hand.

The aquamarine engagement ring...wasn't there.

I had anticipated something like this. I knew that beyond a certain point, there would be worlds where Kazune and I weren't engaged. And World 35 was *well* beyond that point, so the possibility was always there. But when I saw her naked ring finger, I couldn't suppress my shock.

"...Takasaki-kun?" As she frowned dubiously, I silently raised my IP band for her to see. The moment she noticed the number displayed there, her eyes went wide as saucers. "*Thirty-five?!* That's quite a journey... It's the highest I've ever seen!"

This reaction reminded of the time she tricked me in high school. Back then, she had laid a sticker over her IP band screen to convince me she was from World 85. It totally worked—and as a result, we became friends. But what about in this world?

Were those memories gone too? Thankfully, it was her next words that saved me from a panic attack.

"You're not trying to get back at me for what happened in high school, are you?" She reached out and ran a fingernail over the screen. "Doesn't seem to be a sticker... So you *really* shifted across 35 worlds? Where did I say I was from again? Was it World 35?"

What a relief. Those memories still existed here. I didn't know at what point this world had branched off from my past, but it was safe to assume that she and I were still friends. I was too overcome with emotion to speak, but when she noticed my silence, her first thought was the same as mine.

"Did...that not happen in your world?" she asked.

From the concern on her face, I could tell that those memories were as important to her as they were to me, and that really meant a lot.

"...It wasn't 35, it was 85," I said.

"*Eighty-five?* Was it really that far? How in the world did you fall for it, then?"

"Well, I... I didn't know as much about parallel worlds as I do now, obviously..."

"Riiight." She smirked at me. Evidently, Kazune 35's personality was much the same as mine. I hated it, but *god*, I loved it.

"Great work, you two!" a colleague called out, walking past to the door.

"Oh, uh, you too..." I'd forgotten we were loitering right in front of the entrance. "Instead of standing around, would you wanna get something to eat?"

"Hmm... Oh, I know! If we're going out, why not do some karaoke like old times?"

Like old times. Those words made the distance between Kazune and I in this world palpably clear. In mine, we went for karaoke every other week or so.

"Yeah... For old times' sake," I answered carefully.

And so, after we grabbed a quick meal, we went to our usual karaoke lounge. First, we toasted our boozy drinks and sang a few songs to get the stress out. Then our appetizers arrived, so we took a break from singing to catch up.

Personally, I wanted to find out which critical juncture this world had branched from. I could see she and I weren't engaged—were we still dating? Or were we just friends? Just coworkers? Obviously, I was curious.

"Are you seeing anyone right now?"

"No, sadly. What about you? I don't suppose your situation's anything like the one I made up when we were teens, is it?"

"Well, I can tell you I never rescued you from a weirdo in an alley."

"Oh, I remember that part! Mmm, that takes me back," she said with a wistful smile on her face.

Evidently, she was single in this world—we weren't together at all. Would that put the branching point at our first year of college? Back then, she asked me to be her boyfriend so she could avoid excess male attention. Had that not happened in this world? Now that I thought about it, that was the point at which she started calling me Koyomi, so... Yeah, that fit.

TO EVERY YOU I'VE LOVED BEFORE

"So you're saying we have the same sort of relationship 35 entire worlds away? Well, that's not much of a *parallel world*, now is it?"

We'd paid for our drinks, and she was already a little tipsy. Even here, she was still a total lightweight. So what was I supposed to say? I hesitated to admit that we were, in fact, engaged to be wed back in my world—because for some reason, part of me felt like it might have a butterfly effect on this one. Not that I was especially opposed to Kazune and I getting together in this world as well, but...

No, that wasn't it. I very nearly overlooked something important. Why hadn't I thought of it sooner?

"What? Is there a bug in here?" she asked.

"Huh?"

"You've got a glint in your eye like you just spotted something."

"Oh, uh...sorry, it's nothing." She looked at me suspiciously, so I donned my best evasive smile.

"Now tell me, what's the story? What's our relationship in your world?"

"*Welllll*... Some things are better left unsaid."

"Oh, come on!" She pouted her lips.

The reason I was better off not telling her about our engagement in my world was because...Koyomi 35 might be in love with someone else.

Sure, the possibility was infinitesimally small, but it wasn't zero. And if that was the case, then I couldn't risk putting ideas in this Kazune's head. Honestly, the same was true even if

Koyomi 35 *wasn't* in love with someone else. He and Kazune 35 had their own lives to live. I didn't want to blow it all up by dropping a bombshell where it wasn't needed.

"In all seriousness, I'm fairly certain you and I must be dating *somewhere*, you know, out in one of those distant worlds," she said.

"It's possible, yeah."

Yes, in this world, Kazune and I getting together was only a possibility—one that the two of them had perhaps spent many a cold, sleepless night dreaming of. And for me, *this* was a possibility—the possibility of me *not* choosing her, or her *not* choosing me. With my entire being, I represented the possibility of choosing Kazune, and as such, under no circumstances could I reject a world where I didn't.

Just then—

"Oh."

The fog lifted, and I saw my answer clear as day. *Possibilities. Loving someone and all their possibilities!*

"Of course... I get it now!" I said.

"Hm? What's the matter?"

"Oh, I just...had an epiphany, that's all."

"Oh...?" She cocked her head, puzzled, and I started to find her adorable.

Could I marry this Kazune? The answer was clear to me. No. Well, I *could*, but if I truly wanted to marry Kazune, then it wouldn't be *right*.

"Hey, Kazune?"

"What is it?"

"I can't get into the details, but...I'm happy with where my life is headed. Are you?"

"Well...if I had to choose, I suppose I'd say yes."

"Gotcha. Glad to hear it."

I raised my glass to that. And for some reason, I felt the desperate urge to go home and see my Kazune.

• • •

I finally returned to World Zero two days later. After absorbing as much of World 35's research as humanly possible, I got into the IP capsule and had them send me home. My IP went back to 000 without incident.

When I climbed out of the capsule, the researcher who was operating the magnetic field apologized profusely. I was fine with it as I had accepted this risk back when I first consented to take part in the trial. Besides, nothing bad had happened—in fact, the failure provided useful data in its own way. I explained all this in order to put a stop to the apology, because quite frankly, my mind was elsewhere anyway.

In my world, Kazune and I were on the same research team. She was one of the colleagues currently surrounding me. And I knew she had just spent the past two days in close contact with Koyomi 35.

After work, we went home together and had a conversation in the bedroom.

"First off, welcome home," she said.

"Thanks."

"What was I like over there?"

"Hardly any different. Good at singing, bad at booze," I said.

"You went to karaoke?"

"Yeah."

"So did I. Takasaki-kun took me out for old times' sake."

"I suspected as much."

Somehow, I knew they'd make the same choice, and evidently, so had Kazune. We shared a chuckle.

"What did you talk about with him?"

"Oh, we had a lovely discussion about *Does God Play Dice: The New Mathematics of Chaos.*"

"Chaos theory! Nice. Very thematically appropriate too."

"And you? What did you discuss with her?"

"That there's no such thing as wave function collapse."

"The Everett interpretation?" she asked.

"I'm talking about our present and future," I replied with a straight face, and her smile vanished. The whole reason we volunteered to do these optional shift experiments was to answer a single question. Was it still okay to get married even if one of us parallel shifted on the big day?

"I...still haven't found my answer yet," she said after a pause.

"Well, I have."

"Tell me."

The pleading look in her eyes was practically unthinkable coming from a woman who normally carried herself with such confidence.

I smiled back at her. "On our wedding day, we should take our IP bands off."

Her eyes widened. She probably wasn't expecting to hear that.

"That way, it won't matter what our IP is," I continued. "I want to marry you for the human being that you are, the way people have done for thousands of years."

"But...then I won't know who exactly I married..."

"Me. You're going to marry *me*. Every version of me, possibilities and all."

"Possibilities and all...?" She furrowed her brow like she didn't understand what I was saying.

I decided to make use of something she'd mentioned earlier. "Let's say I'm a single die. The instant you toss me, the world splits into six—one for each of my sides. 1 is the one where you and I get married, and the rest are all parallel worlds. With me so far?"

"Yes." She nodded without protest. She always turned quiet and meek whenever she was feeling vulnerable.

"The thing is, you're marrying the *whole die*, not just one side. The others don't stop existing just because the 1 is facing up. If anything, the only reason we're getting married at all is because those other sides exist. Without them, there wouldn't *be* a 1."

She listened to me speak in perfect silence, gazing at me innocently. The version of me in this world was just one small fraction—and I wanted her to love the whole package.

"So let's take off our IP bands. Let's marry each other for *every* side of the die—*all* those possibilities included."

"All those possibilities..." She was sounding more and more convinced.

We couldn't get married at all if it wasn't for the possibilities where we didn't choose each other. That's why I wanted to include them in our marriage.

"Granted, if there's a long-distance shift on the big day and the visitor doesn't want to go through with it, *then* we'll stop the ceremony. But frankly, a shift that huge is next to impossible without the IP capsule, anyway."

"What if it's a close shift, like one or two away...? *That's* not impossible. Then I'd be marrying the Koyomi from a world next door."

"True, but close shifts tend to revert back quickly. And I mean, if the shift is that close, there's basically no difference between our worlds. Would you suddenly no longer want to marry me if I cut my hair? Or if I drove a different car?"

"Of course not," she replied.

"Then it's fine! Every me within close range has chosen to marry you."

"You're completely fine with me marrying a different you from another world?"

"It's just a different side of the same die—Kazune 1 marrying Koyomi 2. But the dice are still getting married at the end of the day. You and I are getting married, period."

"A different side of the same die..."

Judging from the look on her face, 90 percent of her initial fears had been allayed—but that last 10 percent was still there. Thankfully, I had just the tool to wipe it away.

"Kazune."

"Yes?"

"I want to love *every* you. And I want you to love *every* me."

"I know..."

"So, will you marry me?"

"...I will."

I pulled her glasses off and wiped away the single tear that streaked down her face.

• • •

And that was how we decided to marry our possibilities.

Interlude

OWING TO THE DATA acquired from our informal trials, we were granted approval to hold official clinical trials. Three years later, optional shifts were made a reality. Many parallel worlds chose to start their experiments at the same time, fostering the exchange of information, and as a result, the multiverse essentially turned into a giant quantum computer. This in turn led to even more breakthroughs—the ability to observe imaginary elements directly, and with it, the power to stabilize IPs (also known as an IP lock) and other technologies related to controlling movement between worlds.

Naturally, with the abundance of new shift technology, laws governing it were enacted swiftly. After all, criminals stood to gain a great deal from the ability to travel between worlds. If they committed a crime in their home world, they could optional shift somewhere far away, lock their IP, and stay there to easily evade punishment for their crime. The act of pinning a crime on a parallel self would come to be known as IP fraud.

In response, the Japanese government established several new laws as well as a Ministry of Imaginary Technology. All research facilities performing imaginary science experiments were required to register with the Ministry and submit a full log of IP capsule use. Furthermore, new departments were established within Japan's National Police Agency and the Public Prosecutors Office specifically to handle multiverse criminal investigations and prevent IP fraud. Suspects would have their IPs temporarily locked until the end of their trial.

With the advent of the Ministry of Imaginary Science, our laboratory was reclassified as a National Research and Development Agency and was renamed as the Japan National Imaginary Science Research Institute. (A mouthful, to be sure!) After that, we started getting a lot more visits from total strangers, like police detectives and lawyers. The increased amount of paperwork and other boring tasks consumed a lot of time otherwise spent actually researching things—but our bolstered salaries made things a lot easier for our families, so it wasn't all bad.

At that time, optional shifting and IP locking weren't part of everyday life for most people. However, its implementation was spreading like wildfire, and it wouldn't be long before private-sector corporations started offering it as a household service. Society was struggling to keep up with this rapidly evolving technology.

But as the rest of the world grappled with a massive paradigm shift, Kazune and I spent our newlywed days in peace. Sure, we had our little spats here and there, but for the most part we got along swimmingly. On the other hand, as a child of divorce, every time my mother commented on how "lucky" we were to have each other, I wasn't really sure how to feel.

The world was hurtling at breakneck speed into a new era, yet neither of us experienced any major parallel shifts outside of those experiments we took part in. Life was good. And during the second year of our marriage, we had a son who we named Ryou. We chose the kanji of his name to symbolize crisp spring water—a foundation for life's blessing, an origin point, and a good home.

My only real complaint was that Kazune spoiled Ryou too much and didn't seem to have as much time for me anymore, but *obviously* I knew it was extremely pathetic for a grown man to get jealous of his own son. I did my best to hide it.

Fortunately, as Ryou grew older, Kazune's obsession with him calmed down, and my mother agreed to babysit him so we could finally go on dates again. Now it was Ryou's turn to get jealous of *me* for "stealing" his mommy. He made it a point to barge in on us as much as possible, and whenever he and I got into little tug-of-war battles over Kazune, she would shake her head at us with a smile.

It was those little mundane moments that truly meant the world to me.

• • •

TO EVERY YOU I'VE LOVED BEFORE

And then, the year before Ryou started first grade, Kazune and I were struck with the greatest calamity of our lives.

CHAPTER 4

Middle Age

NEW YEAR'S DAY. I was hoping to spend at least *one* holiday relaxing at home, but once again, Kazune and Ryou shook me awake first thing in the morning to go celebrate Hatsumode at our local shrine. My wife and I visited this shrine together as part of our yearly tradition, but this year, we were bringing Ryou for the first time.

When she suggested we could go to Usa Jingu this year instead to celebrate the milestone, I balked. As the first-ever Hachiman shrine, Usa Jingu had gone on to inspire 40,000 branch shrines nationwide. Naturally, it received hundreds of thousands of visitors every year. Those crowds were pure hell; we did it once before, and I wasn't eager to repeat the experience. When I reminded her how frustrating and exhausting it was—and how badly we both needed to pee the whole time—she mercifully agreed that we should stick to our usual Inari shrine.

That being said, our usual was still a large shrine in its own right. We took the scenic route through the mountains, avoiding the congested highways, and by the time we arrived, the entrance path was already choked with visitors. It got about a tenth of the foot traffic that Usa Jingu did, but that was still nothing to sneeze at.

Ryou had never seen so many people in one place before and was bouncing with excitement. "Daddy! Look at all the people!"

"Yep, lots of people here. Don't let go of our hands, okay?"

"Your father's right, Ryou. Make sure you hold on tight," my wife said.

To ensure no one would get separated, Kazune and I positioned ourselves on either side of Ryou and progressed slowly through the crowd with our hands joined. We passed through dozens of torii gates, climbed up hundreds of stairs, and by the time we finally reached the hall of worship, it was nearly half an hour later. I couldn't complain—the same process would have taken over an hour at Usa Jingu. At last, we walked up to the offering box, and I pulled out the money I prepared in advance.

"Ryou, how about you ring that bell for us two or three times?"

"Okay!" He gleefully rang the bell as hard as he could.

Then, once the three of us put our offerings into the box, it was time for the traditional ritual: bow twice, clap twice, bow once. Ryou did his very best to follow along with us, and it was quite precious, if I do say so myself.

"Daddy, what did you wish for?"

We had taught him that people go to shrines in order to make wishes. Sure, it wasn't completely accurate, but eh, close enough.

Granted, I was always told wishes only came true if you kept yours a secret, but in this case, I decided not to worry about it.

"Daddy wished for you and Mommy and Grandma to always be in good health."

"What about you, Mommy?"

"The same thing, of course. I wished for you and Daddy and Grandma to be healthy. And you?"

"Um... I wished that we could have Salisbury steak for dinner!"

"*Again?* You really love Mommy's Salisbury steak, don't you?" I laughed.

I liked it a lot myself, but we already ate it on a weekly basis. Any more than that probably wasn't healthy. Granted, Kazune *did* seem to be making an effort to keep our dinners nutritionally balanced, so while I wanted to gradually wean her off of spoiling him so much, I couldn't find it in me to protest too strongly.

"Hey Mommy, what's that drink?"

"It's called amazake. Have you ever had it?"

"No!"

"You haven't? Koyomi, should we let him?"

"Is amazake safe for kids? I don't remember."

We flagged down a shrine maiden to ask, then stood in line to receive our kid-safe amazake. Since it was a drink made from fermented rice, some of it was alcoholic, but the shrine sold one that wasn't as well. Anyway, Ryou didn't seem to like it much sadly. The boy took one sip and grimaced.

After doing our prayers, heading away from the shrine grounds and toward home was a breeze. On our way out, food stalls peeked through the thinning crowds, and naturally Ryou took an immediate interest. I was feeling a little hungry myself too.

"Wanna get some food, Kazune?"

"Good question... Are you hungry, Ryou?"

"Yeah!"

"Okay, let's get a little something, then."

With her blessing, I looked around at our options. Festival food could get a little overpriced, so I needed to stay sharp. Letting go of Ryou's hand, I stopped and checked what I had in my wallet. Meanwhile, he eagerly dragged Kazune off to the food stalls.

And that was when a commotion broke out on the path.

The first thing I heard was murmuring in the crowd. Curious, I looked over to see what was happening. The line of shrinegoers was disorganized, and everyone was looking in the same direction, into the center of the crowd. I couldn't see much from where I was.

Then, out of nowhere, I heard a man's enraged roar...and a woman's scream.

Instantly, the crowd rippled, and people pushed each other like dominoes down a narrow pathway. Those who made it through headed to the food stall plaza for safety. And as the wall of people split, I glimpsed a lone man standing there. At least, I assumed it was a man, but he was wearing sunglasses and a face mask, so I couldn't be sure.

In his right hand, he clutched a blade that was glistening red.

Screaming wildly, he came charging down the path, waving his weapon. In a blink, his unconcealed malice had warped this peaceful holiday into something straight out of my worst nightmare. I looked around for my family, from whom I was now separated...and my heart nearly stopped.

The man was headed straight for Kazune and Ryou.

His screams grew louder—I think he was saying "Move!"—but frankly, it didn't matter.

The crowd shrieked. The man bellowed. Kazune dropped to her knees, shielding Ryou with her whole body.

The blade. The red. My legs moved. Fear. Confusion. Anger.

Ryou! Kazune!

I barreled forward blindly and slammed myself into the man with the knife.

• • •

A tragic shrine attack on New Year's Day. There were no fatalities, but several were injured, so the story was covered nationwide. Like always, they speculated that the culprit was a mentally ill lone wolf, rejected by society and influenced by too much violent media. But more than that—according to his testimony, he "just wanted to hurt someone and didn't care who." As his victims, *that* was what frightened us most of all.

Although Japan was said to have a comparatively low crime rate, I knew things like this still happened from time to time. I just never imagined it would happen to *us*.

The one silver lining was that no one died. The three of us were unharmed too. After I ran in and tackled the guy, a bunch of men from the crowd leapt in and pinned him to the ground.

Then someone called the cops, and I didn't want to get involved with all that, so I took Kazune and Ryou and got the hell out of there.

On the way home, Kazune held Ryou in her arms the entire time. He didn't seem to understand how close he came to getting hurt; instead, he blithely shrugged it off. "That was crazy!" he had said.

Then again, anything was better than him being traumatized.

By the time we arrived at home, the attack was already all over the news, and my mother came running to greet us. "Thank god you're home! Is anyone hurt?!"

"We're fine, Mom. We were on the other side of the shrine when it happened."

"Ryou's fine too. Nothing to worry about."

To keep Mom from worrying herself into an early grave, we agreed to tell her we were nowhere near the scene of the crime, and that we left as soon as the commotion broke out. If she knew I'd charged at the culprit myself, she'd have a heart attack.

Later that night, however, Kazune sat me down for a real scolding.

"Which do you want first?" she asked. "Good cop or bad cop?"

She started all her lectures this way to let me know I was in for it. At this point, there was no getting out of it.

"Bad cop, I think."

I made the same choice every time. If she was going to get angry with me, then I at least wanted her to console me with kindness afterwards.

"All right then. Now look here—it is far, *far* too dangerous to tackle someone who's holding a knife! In case no one ever told you, you don't have the athletic reflexes for that! I never want you risking yourself like that ever again! Think of what it would do to our son if anything happened to you!"

The birth of Ryou had changed Kazune. If I had to guess why, it was probably because he had become her new number one priority in life. As her husband, it was hard to reconcile that, but as Ryou's father, nothing could make me happier.

Therefore, I didn't protest. Sure, I could have said, "if I hadn't taken action, the two of you would have been in danger," but that was only an excuse. As Ryou's father, the correct choice of action was to find a way to protect him and his mother *without* putting myself at risk.

"I know. I'm sorry."

"Have you learned your lesson?"

"Yes," I said.

"You won't risk yourself ever again?"

Now *that* I couldn't guarantee. I was no comic book super-hero, so if something like that ever happened to us again, my only option would be to risk my own life to save theirs.

"I'll...try," I answered.

She stared daggers back at me without a word. The silence lingered between us. We'd been through a few wordless nights in the past—nights where we had just enough good sense to keep our mouths shut—but we weren't young twenty-somethings anymore.

Kazune let out a small sigh. The tension eased. "Time for good cop."

No sooner had the words left her mouth than she pulled me into a hug, cradling my head against her chest.

"Thank you for saving me. You were so manly."

"You're welcome. Fell in love with me all over again, did you?"

"Yes, I did. Remember what I told you?" she asked.

"What?"

"I love a man who can charge in to rescue me from a weirdo."

"Oh yeah..." I said, reminiscing. "Man, that takes me back."

"I feel like a teenager again, don't you?"

"Wanna try on your old high school uniform?"

"Hush!"

But her rebuke was as soft as the lips she pressed to mine.

• • •

That incident may not have killed anyone, but the damage was done—particularly to Kazune's mental health.

Our New Year's holiday would last for the next three days. After that, we would go back to work, and Ryou would go back to kindergarten... At least, he was *supposed* to. But Kazune could no longer handle being apart from him.

"C'mon, there's nothing to worry about. He'll be fine."

"But what if something like that happens again?!"

No matter what I said to her, she stubbornly refused to detach herself from him. Could I really blame her? I could only imagine how it must have felt to watch a crazed man come charging straight at her with a blood-soaked knife. One wrong move and that weapon could have ended her life—or our son's. I understood why she was so anxious.

Thus, I contacted the lab and Ryou's school, letting them know we needed a few extra days for Kazune to feel secure again. She was a rational person; after a few days of peace, surely her emotions would stabilize, and she'd be fine again.

"Okay, Kazune, I contacted the school and the lab. Just take it easy and relax with Ryou for a few more days."

"Okay... Sorry about this, Koyomi. Thank you for under-standing."

She smiled weakly, and I cursed myself for lacking the power to allay her fears. But as her husband and the father of her son, the best I could do for her was to go to work in her stead. So that's precisely what I did.

Two days passed, then three, then four.

But after a full week, Kazune still showed no signs of improvement.

On my day off from work, I watched TV with my mother while Kazune was off playing a game with Ryou in his bedroom. According to Mom, Kazune had been hovering over him *nonstop* this past week. She was still keeping up with her housework, and by keeping our son within arm's reach at all times, he had learned how to help out with some chores too. That much was all well and good, but...

"The boy's *fine*. He's a little ball of energy, and he wants to go outside and play. But Kazune-chan... She worries me. Now, I don't blame her, given what could have happened, but... Frankly, she's blowing it way out of proportion."

Mom didn't know that the culprit had targeted Kazune and Ryou; we had lied to her about it to prevent her from getting paranoid herself. So in her eyes, it must have looked like Kazune was just being dramatic.

"And she even cut herself with a knife while cooking? I'm just saying, it might be good for her to speak to a therapist at least once."

A few days prior, I came home from work to find Kazune with her left wrist bandaged up. She told me she accidentally dropped a knife while cooking and cut herself pretty badly. Since the bandages were still there several days later, the wound must have been fairly deep. If she kept slipping up like that, she could injure herself even worse, or Ryou could be hurt. That was the exact opposite of what she wanted.

But something told me it would only make things worse if I tried to push her to seek therapy out of nowhere. Instead, I decided I'd stick with my original plan for the day and have another long talk with her. I let Mom know, then I headed off to Ryou's room.

"Right there, Ryou! Get over there!"

"Quit nagging, Mommy!"

Through the door, I could hear Kazune and Ryou shouting excitedly to each other. From their voices, you'd almost think everything was fine.

"I'm coming in!" I called as I entered.

Inside the room, Ryou was wearing a headset and playing a VR game while Kazune cheered him on. On the external monitor, I could see it was a soccer game.

"What is it, Koyomi?"

"Well, I kinda need to talk to you."

"About?"

"How about we step into our room real quick?"

"Can't we talk here?"

"I need to speak to you in private."

"But..."

She glanced furtively at Ryou. Meanwhile, he carried on playing his video game like he couldn't even hear us. I waited for him to reach a good stopping point, then gave him a little pat on the shoulder.

"Ryou, put that on pause, buddy."

He pulled off his headset and looked at me in confusion.

"Daddy needs to talk to Mommy for a little while," I continued. "You can play VR again later."

"Awwww! But Daddyyyy..." He pouted his lips at me.

In our household, Ryou wasn't allowed to play VR without adult supervision. The realistic 3D worlds were so engrossing that real-world accidents were all too common, and I could tell that was what Kazune was worried about.

"Just play a game on the TV screen."

"But VR's easier!"

Sign of the times, I suppose. When I was a boy, VR was something only rich people had access to. But just ten years later, it became the top Christmas gift for kids. Those days, when people said "video games," they meant VR by default. The standards of "normal" were prone to change over time, and at that point, the concept of playing games on a monitor was outright foreign to most kids. Then again, perhaps the evolution of video game technology was nothing compared to how quickly and drastically imaginary science had changed the whole world.

"All right, Daddy's confiscating your HMD for a bit. You'll get it back once we're done talking. And let us know if you decide to play outside, okay?"

"Okaaay..."

Though he didn't look happy about it, he still obeyed, and I was relieved to know that we were raising him right.

"Be safe, Ryou. Don't do anything dangerous."

"Mommy, you're so naggy now!"

"It's for your own good! The world's not a safe place!" Kazune spat, angry that he was brushing off her concern. She had never shouted at him like this before, and I could see a hint of fear growing in his petulant eyes.

"Wow, Mommy sure is nagging a lot. But our Ryou's gonna be just fine! He'd never do something unsafe. Isn't that right, son?" I said in a playful voice as I ruffled his hair, hoping to keep that tiny seed of trepidation toward his mother from taking root. "C'mon, Mommy, you know what you ought to say. '*I'm starry.*'"

Kazune paused for a moment. "Don't be ridiculous... Ryou, I'm safari."

"It's SORRY!" our son retorted with perfect timing.

Frankly, I was glad to see that Kazune still had it in her to play along with my joke. We all shared a laugh, and then she and I headed off to the grown-ups' room.

• • •

Once we were in private, however, that tiny smile faded.

"Kazune."

"I know..."

"Look, I get how you feel. I know how much you love him, and I know that's why you're scared something bad might happen again. But...I don't want him to be chained down by our fears."

She didn't speak, so I continued.

"I admit, there's always a level of risk. What happened on New Year's—the chances of that scenario were infinitesimally small, and yet it still happened. Looking at it that way, it might seem safer to stay together 24/7 and never set foot outside the house again. But if you ask me, it's worth the price of admission to live our lives in the outside world. Every day is a gamble, but we all take that 1 percent of risk! If I stayed cooped up in my house because I was afraid of car accidents, I never would have met you, and Ryou never would have been born! We can't rob him of those exact same happy possibilities."

Over the past few days, I had spent a lot of time thinking about what exactly to say to her. I didn't want to hurt her, but something needed to give. I decided to take the angle of Ryou's best interests and what he stood to lose from her paranoia.

I wanted him to have a life just as good—no, *better* than I had. And if she loved him like I did, then surely she'd feel the same.

However...

"You..." Her voice trembled along with her shoulders. "You only think that because you're alive, Koyomi. Trust me, I know. Yes, happiness is worth a little risk—I agree with that. But...that's only because we're both *alive*...!"

Her body started to shake harder, and I started to think maybe I didn't understand how she felt nearly as well as I thought I did. Admittedly, I hadn't realistically considered the risk of death, and that was probably because I managed to defend Ryou from the threat that day. Deep down, it had convinced me that the next time something bad happened, I could protect him again, even though I had no guarantee. From her point of view, perhaps this was a reckless attitude to take.

"You only feel that way because the 99 percent success rate has never done you wrong. But what about that *1 percent*? If there's always one out of a hundred who pulls the short straw, then...is it so wrong to choose not to pull at all?"

I paused before answering. "Well, statistically, it seems like an awful shame to pass on a 99 percent chance of success out of fear of the last 1 percent—"

She grabbed my collar with both hands. "And I'm telling you that *you* can only say that because you've never gambled and lost!"

Behind her glasses, I could see tears welling up. Her eyes were full of despair, like they'd seen the darkest depths of hell itself. And the way she put that emphasis on a certain word...

Something just wasn't right. Why would she be so afraid of that 1 percent risk?

You can only say that because you've never gambled and lost. The way she phrased it, she made it sound like she *had* lost that gamble—

Just then, for some reason I can't explain, my eyes were suddenly drawn to the white bandage wrapped around her left wrist. As I recalled, she was injured five days ago; I remembered coming home from work and being shocked to see the bandage. She said she wrapped it herself with her other hand and that's why it was clumsy. In fact, it had looked an awful lot like it did now.

No...it was *exactly* the same.

Five days ago, she bandaged up her injury...and then she just left it as it was? Without changing it? Would she *really* do that?

"Kazune." I grabbed her left arm.

She gasped. "No, don't...!"

She squirmed and tried to shake me off. Being a man, I was stronger than she was. I yanked her arm close and unwrapped the bandages.

Underneath...there was no wound.

Instantly, I felt the resistance drain from her slender arm, and she slumped her shoulders without a word.

Why would she bandage herself if there was no wound? To hide something? If so, what? What could she need to hide on her left wrist?

"Kazune," I began again, "where's your IP band?"

Defeated, she meekly pointed to the vanity drawer. When I opened it, sure enough, I found an IP band hidden under her other things. I pulled it out and put it back on her wrist.

I powered it on, and the display read...013.

"Since when?" I asked quietly.

"...A week ago."

One week ago—that was right when winter break ended and Kazune first started getting really anxious about Ryou. But that wasn't *my* Kazune at all, was it? The paranoia, the helicopter parenting—it was all Kazune from World 13. And to prevent us from finding out, she pretended to have hurt herself so she could take her IP band off without suspicion. She then proceeded to spend the next week straight with Ryou. But why?

You can only say that because you've never gambled and lost.

There could be only one answer.

"Kazune... In your world, did he...?"

"...That's right."

I didn't want to hear this...but...

"In my world...he was stabbed by that criminal... And he *died*!"

Tears streamed from her eyes. Her voice was halfway between a hiss and a whisper—probably to keep our Ryou from hearing—but I could tell she wanted to scream and curse the world into oblivion. Her body shook hard as she clenched her teeth, choking the sobs down, yet a few whimpers escaped. They tore my heart into shreds.

But all I could do was stand there and gaze down at the top of her head.

"It's not *fair*, damn you...! Just thirteen worlds away...*your* Ryou gets to live...and play, and be *happy*...!"

This time, I was certain beyond a doubt. Under no uncertain terms did I "get how she felt," and I regretted ever saying otherwise.

I couldn't *possibly* know how she felt. My entire argument was based on the fact that Ryou survived. If I had watched him die right in front of my eyes...I'd sure as hell never utter a word of that bull.

But Kazune *had* watched him die. She must have optional shifted here, to a world where he was alive. In rejection of the world where he wasn't. And as a result...

Oh god.

That's when I realized—if Kazune 13 was here, then *my* Kazune was trapped in a world where our son was dead.

"Kazune...!"

She must have known that I wasn't calling for her, because Kazune 13 didn't respond. Taking a deep, steadying breath, I put a hand on her shoulder.

"Kazune... Did you optional shift here?"

She nodded silently.

"Why is that?" I asked, as gently as possible.

She didn't seem to want to answer this, but I wasn't going to press her on it. I didn't blame her whatsoever. Hadn't she been through enough? If my world's Kazune was the 1 face of a die, then this was her 6. They were both the same die. And I had vowed to love every her with every me.

"...I..."

At last, she began to speak. *It's okay,* I mouthed as I stroked her hair.

"I wanted to...see him..."

I know.

"I wanted to see him...one last time...!"

That was where the dam burst. She pulled off her glasses and began to wail openly, wiping tear after endless tear. Mom and Ryou could probably hear her now, but I was in no position to ask her not to cry. The most I could offer her was a tight hug, rubbing her back as she sobbed like a child.

I thought about my next move. I would sooner tear my own face off than tell this Kazune to run back home. But in World 13 where Ryou was dead, *my* Kazune was sure to be grieving him too. I couldn't just leave her there.

The closer a given parallel world was to your home world, the more frequently you'd shift to it, and the faster you'd shift back home. Conversely, the farther a world was, the less often you'd shift to it, and if you *did* end up there, it'd take a while to get back. World 13 was somewhere in the middle of these two extremes: not that close, but hardly far. Part of me felt like they might shift back on their own without me meddling—

"Mommy?" Just then, the door opened, and Ryou timidly peeked his head in. "Daddy? Why is Mommy sad?"

As soon as she heard Ryou's voice, I felt Kazune's arms tense around me. I gave her a reassuring little pat while I answered, "Oh, Mommy's got a real bad stomachache. Could you come over and help her feel better?"

"Your tummy hurts?" Ryou came running right over to the bed, sat down next to Kazune, and reached out to her stomach. "Are you okay, Mommy?"

"Oh, Ryou..." She looked up, her face wet with tears, and gingerly stroked his hair. "Thank you, honey... You're so sweet..."

"Don't cry, Mommy," he told her, though the look in his eyes suggested he might burst into sobs right along with her. "See, when you do this, the pain goes away." He put his hand on her stomach and gently rubbed up and down, just as she always did for him whenever he had a stomachache. "How's that? Feel better?"

"Yeah... I really do... Thank you, Ryou..."

Wiping her tears, she smiled at him...and I took that as my cue to step out of the room. Part of me wanted to give them a little more time together, and another part of me wanted to go reassure my mother that everything was okay. When I arrived in the living room, I found Mom staring blankly into space with the TV off.

"Mom?"

"Oh, Koyomi... How's Kazune-chan?"

"She's okay now. Ryou's looking after her," I replied, though in hindsight I wasn't sure what exactly I meant by *okay*.

"All right, well—"

Before she could finish, however, a phone call came in. I looked at her, and she chuckled and gestured for me to answer it. I checked the screen.

"It's Dad...? Sorry, Mom, I should take this." I directed my attention to the phone. "Hello?"

"Hey, Koyomi. Got time to talk?" my father asked over the line.

"Yeah, what's up?"

"Sorry for the short notice, but could you and Kazune-kun come to the lab ASAP?"

"Right now? Kazune too? What's going on?"

The laboratory was open 365 days a year and employees took days off on rotation. It wasn't unheard of for them to call me in like this, but I could tell from my father's voice that something was amiss.

"Well, you see..."

The next words out of his mouth were beyond my wildest imagination.

• • •

After I put Mom on babysitting duty and convinced Kazune to come with me to the lab, we found Dad and the director waiting for us.

Over the phone, Dad had told me our IPs were locked—mine and Kazune's. Normally, the only time someone's IP was locked without their consent was when they were involved in some sort of crime. The only crime I could think of was the incident on New Year's, but the cops already had the guy—so if it wasn't that, then what else could it be? When I asked Dad for details, however, he told me he'd explain everything in person.

Hence why the four of us were now sitting in this soundproof meeting room with the door locked and our phones in airplane mode.

"To put it simply, your parallel selves are prime suspects in a murder case."

"...*What?*"

It struck me like a bolt of lightning, and Kazune's eyes went as wide as saucers.

"The locks went into effect last night, and the cops delivered the paperwork this morning. They say the murder took place two nights ago with a relative SIP of 22, plus or minus 10. Granted, with a range like that, normally you wouldn't be involved at all, but..."

SIP was short for Schwarzschild IP, which referred to the range within which a given event was ensured to take place inside each parallel world. An SIP of 22 ± 10 meant that, relative to our World Zero, the event had taken place across worlds 12 through 32, with World 22 at the center. And since 0 was outside that range, yes, one would think our world wasn't involved. But my father wasn't finished speaking...and I could guess what he was about to say.

"Record of an unauthorized optional shift was discovered within that very same SIP, traveling a distance of 13 worlds. And the shifter was you, wasn't it, Kazune-kun?"

"...Yes."

Indeed, this Kazune had an IP of 13, which just barely fell into that SIP range. It was hard to say she was entirely unrelated.

"We gathered all the information we could before you got here. The murder took place two nights ago, between the hours of 8 p.m. and 11 p.m. The scene of the crime varies from world to world. Take a look at this map." He unfolded an old-fashioned paper map. Our home address was marked on it, as well as a handful of other numbered spots. "These are all the crime scenes across the entire SIP."

I looked at each one in turn. Some were buildings, some were alleys, some were public parks. The only thing they seemed to have in common was their relative proximity to our house. But more importantly...

"Are you absolutely sure about this one?" I asked, pointing to one of the buildings marked on the map.

Dad grimaced, then nodded. "Yes, we triple-checked that one. It's your house, all right."

In a parallel world, my own house was the scene of a murder?

"You're joking... *Why*...?"

"Well, when you see the victim, you might get your answer."

Next, he laid out a profile sheet with a photograph of what I assumed was the murder victim: a woman in her forties. I didn't recognize her face, and her name didn't sound that familiar, either...at first.

"Wait... That surname..."

"Yep. The New Year's stabber? This is his wife."

One by one, the puzzle pieces were coming together...though I didn't want them to.

"In our world there were no fatalities, but about 20 worlds away...I'm told Ryou was killed. Naturally, the story was about a thousand times more viral there, so your house was all over the news. That was how the killer's wife learned your address. Then, two nights ago, she visited in person to apologize..."

And then she was murdered. Given the circumstances, it was no wonder Kazune and I were the prime suspects. In a range of parallel worlds not too far from here, my son Ryou was stabbed to death. Then, another murder happened across a smaller cluster within that same range, at *my house*, and the victim was *the stabber's wife*. The number one suspect was obviously—

"I'm told the cops are looking at our Kazune-kun as their number one."

"What?! Why her?!"

My prediction was wrong in the worst possible way. Surely the evidence pointed to *me*, not her! Nearly all the Kazunes currently within that SIP range had shifted there against their will from worlds where Ryou never died. In short, they had no motive. Plus, the Kazunes who caused the shifts—the ones who lost their sons—most likely only did so out of grief for Ryou. In a way, they were victims too!

"No, that can't be right! My Kazune didn't *choose* to shift there! What motive could she possibly have?! It'd make more sense if—!"

If the murderer had fled here. I choked the words back down right before I let them slip. That wasn't something I had any business blurting out thoughtlessly.

"Settle down, Koyomi. There's a reason they're looking at her. Part of it's because the murder happened after she shifted there, but more importantly, it's because of her alibi."

"What, so...she's the only one who doesn't have one?" I asked.

"On the contrary—in almost all cases, she's the only one who *does* have one. But upon formal investigation, most of those have fallen through."

What the hell? He made it sound like...like Kazune faked her alibi or something!

"In each of the parallel worlds, her alibi is predominantly based on your testimony. But cops don't trust testimony from family, so they looked into it...and found proof of you forging evidence to substantiate it."

"...I can't believe it..."

So in summary...after Ryou was killed in a parallel world, a grieving Kazune fled here, to a world where he was still alive. In exchange, my Kazune was sent to the world without Ryou, learned of his murder...and a few nights later, upon receiving a visit from the killer's wife...killed her? Then my parallel self tried to protect her with a fake alibi, but the cops saw through it, and now she's the prime suspect?

"That... That's *ridiculous*!" Before I knew it, I had slammed my fist on the table. "Kazune can't possibly be the killer! She has no motive! She—!"

Still has her son. But I didn't dare say those words in front of Kazune 13.

"The Gate of Einzwach."

At first, I didn't realize who had spoken...until...

"Director?" my father murmured. *What did she just say? Einzwach?*

"By passing through the gate, even the purest and most innocent will turn into cold-hearted killers. A novelist proposed its existence a few decades back."

This whole time, she sat staring down at the table like this conversation bored her to tears. What did this "Gate of Einzwach" have to do with anything? Was she trying to say Kazune had passed through it? As if! Humans couldn't change overnight!

The director glanced up, and her bottomless eyes bored into me.

"...Okay, well, unlock our IPs," I shot back. "We need to get our Kazune back and talk to her."

"Koyomi, you know we can't do that without police authorization," said Dad.

"Sure you can. You're just not *supposed* to."

"As director, I don't think I can allow it," the director chimed in. "Too much of a hassle all around."

With the ISRI's two highest authority figures opposed to it, it wasn't going to happen. But what else was I supposed to do?

"For right now, go ahead and take some time off from work. We'll let you know if we learn anything. Just stay calm and wait."

Stay calm? How was I supposed to *stay calm* in a situation like this?

The most I was permitted was to make photocopies of the police records to take home with me, so that's what I did...all the while wrestling with my love for Kazune 0 and Kazune 13.

• • •

The hours ticked by, and I still couldn't sleep.

Kazune 13 had shifted here one week ago. She was already here when the murder took place and therefore couldn't be the culprit. The police had thoroughly examined the optional shift records, so that much was fact. And yet, in my anger, I suspected her all the same. That was absolutely unacceptable. With each passing second, I was more and more grateful I managed to stop myself from saying it out loud.

In short: Kazune 13 was not the culprit. The next suspect, then, was Koyomi 13. Having lost his son, he had plenty of motive. But...if he was the culprit, why did he concoct a fake alibi for Kazune?

One possible answer was that he could foresee that Kazune would fall under suspicion, and he wanted to protect her from being falsely accused. According to the police records, however, Koyomi 13 denied any involvement in the murder. If he truly wanted to protect Kazune, the best option would be to give her an alibi *and* confess to the murder. But no—instead, he pointed the finger at a third party.

In World 13, my house was known to the whole country as "the stabber's victim's house." Koyomi 13 had argued that anyone could have seen the stabber's wife standing outside the house and decided to play vigilante in the name of justice. Not *impossible*, per se, but it was so wildly implausible that it made it all the more obvious he was covering for someone. But if so, then that "someone" had to be Kazune 0...and yet I couldn't see *any* way that my Kazune could possibly be the true culprit.

The night after I tackled the stabber, she said to me, "*Think of what it would do to our son if anything happened to you.*" In her mind, she always put Ryou first. There was simply no way she'd murder someone in a parallel world—not if she wanted to go home to her son!

That left only one other possibility. And aside from one point, it would explain all the strange circumstances.

Was Koyomi 13...trying to *frame* Kazune 0?

"Koyomi?" a voice called softly. I turned to find Kazune peeking into the living room, looking at me with concern. "What are you doing still awake?"

I could have asked her the same. "I can't sleep."

"...Thinking about the case?"

She walked over, sat down, and slid her legs under the kotatsu table. And as she gazed at me silently, I found myself opening up to her.

"I just can't see Kazune as the killer. But if *Koyomi's* the killer... then I can only assume he's trying to pin the crime on her. And I hate the thought of me doing that to you, no matter what world it's in." As much as I wanted to think it through rationally, my emotions wouldn't let me.

"I wouldn't want to believe Koyomi could do such a thing, either. He told me he'd love every me and all my possibilities—I can't imagine he'd *ever* be cruel to a Kazune."

That was something I said to my Kazune too. In the end, Koyomi 13 was still me.

"...More importantly..." she started.

"Hm?"

That was when I noticed that she was struggling to tell me something.

"...I..." She couldn't seem to get the words out.

Instead of rushing her, I sat there in silence and waited for her to continue.

Then, at last, she continued. "I think...I could have...killed her."

My first reaction was *what?*

Right—this Kazune had lost her son, so maybe she could have killed the stabber's wife. She had the motive. I knew all that from the beginning...but...

"I know for a fact you didn't do it," I said. "You've been *here* for the past week. You couldn't possibly have murdered someone in World 13 two days ago."

"No, that's not what I'm saying."

Then what *was* she saying? "*I could have killed her...*" Was she trying to say Kazune 0 definitely didn't do it since she had no motive?

"If I was from this world...and if I was sent to a world where my son was murdered... I think that might be enough...to make me kill that woman."

...*Excuse me?* Was she saying a Kazune whose Ryou was still alive would be driven to murder upon discovering a world where he died? She made it sound like...like...

"Are you saying my Kazune's the killer?" I asked.

"No! That's not it. But...I think...the possibility is there."

My mind went white—and I started seeing red.

Are you stupid? My sweet Kazune would NEVER kill someone! I shouldn't have taken you seriously, you witch! My Kazune hasn't lost her son—you can't assume you know a thing about how she feels! You're not her! Why did you even come here? We were happy before you showed up! WE WERE HAPPY! But then you sent my wife to a world where our son is dead, and now she's suspected for murder, and her IP is locked! What if those suspicions are never cleared? Will Kazune 0 be arrested in World 13, never to come home again, while YOU get to play the role of the happy mother? Get the hell out! Why should she—why should WE have to give up our happiness to some random Kazune we don't even—!

Just then, I realized that Kazune 13 was looking at me with sorrow in her eyes.

Instantly, I felt my whole body break out into a sweat. What... what in the world was I thinking just moments before? I had vowed to love every her and *all* her possibilities—the whole die, not just one side of it! Were those thoughts my idea of love? Or was I glaring at her with hatred in my heart, thinking only of my Kazune with no compassion for this one?

"Oh shit." That selfish, hypocritical anger I just felt...had given me an epiphany. "It can't be..."

Parallel shifting. Optional shifting. Kazune 0 and Kazune 13. IP lock. Murder. My parallel self. The vow to love every Kazune—the vow I'd forgotten.

"Kazune?"

"Huh?"

"I'm sorry." All I could offer her was an apology.

"For what?" she asked, confused.

Why was I sorry? Because I'd struck upon the incredibly selfish truth of this case.

"I know who killed her."

• • •

A week later, Kazune's IP was unlocked, and we all gathered in the ISRI shift room to switch them back.

Kazune 13 lay inside the IP capsule. She had just finished spending another full week away from work in order to stay home and coddle Ryou. I suspected that was because she knew she would have to go home soon, so I didn't criticize her for it. I had regained some level of compassion for her, and besides, I didn't feel like I had the right.

"It seems you were correct," she said to me before the glass door closed.

I'd gone to the police to share what I knew about the culprit. That information spread across the parallel worlds. And then yesterday, we received word from World 13 that the true culprit had been uncovered.

It was, of course, my parallel self—Koyomi 13.

This is how it all went down.

After Ryou was murdered, the grieving Kazune shifted away to a world where he was still alive. In her place, Kazune 0 learned of Ryou's death in World 13.

A few days later, the killer's wife came to the house late at night to apologize. And that was when my parallel self killed her. In some worlds, it happened right then and there. In others, it was after she walked off down the street. It was a crime of passion.

He knew that if he made Kazune 0 look suspicious, her IP would be locked. That would ensure Kazune 13 couldn't immediately be sent home in an IP capsule for a good long while, at least not until the end of the investigation—and in turn, she could have lots of happy moments with Ryou.

He gave Kazune 0 a shoddy alibi on purpose, knowing it would fall apart under the slightest scrutiny. Sure enough, it did, and once the cops decided Takasaki Koyomi was covering for his wife, she became the prime suspect.

"How did you figure it out all of a sudden?" Kazune asked me.

I hadn't revealed to anyone how I arrived at the answer, but with Kazune, I wanted to be as honest as possible.

"The night you suggested my Kazune could have a motive... I despised you." Indeed, I inadvertently felt hatred toward one of Kazune's other sides. "At the time, I was only thinking of Kazune 0. I'd forgotten all about my vow to love every you."

She didn't say a word and just listened to me speak.

"Then, I realized... If *I* could forget it, then Koyomi 13 might have forgotten it too. He might have taken action solely to protect *his* Kazune, especially since he already lost his son. He couldn't possibly think rationally after that." I was so sure humans couldn't possibly change overnight, but then I went and proved it to myself. That was how I realized Koyomi 13 must have changed too. "When I thought about the lengths he might go to for you, I realized the truth. He'd make you happy at *any cost*—innocent people like Kazune 0 be damned."

In two different worlds, I had found a way to accidentally

love the only side of the die I could see—*my* Kazune and no one else's.

"How incredibly selfish of him," she sighed. "Seems we might be getting a divorce when I get home."

"I won't ask you to forgive him, but, if possible...could you hold off for a while?"

"In that case, I want you to make that vow again," she said to me.

"Okay. I vow to love you for every side of the die, all your possibilities included."

"...Good. I suppose I could forgive him, then."

"You'd better remind *him* of our vow too."

"Oh, I'm not worried. You're two sides of the same die, remember?" She smiled ever so faintly, then whispered, "I'm going home."

• • •

We closed the capsule lid, then set the magnetic field to IP 13. All the other nearby worlds were probably doing the same thing right about now.

Optional shifts only took a few seconds of closing your eyes. Technically, you could leave them open, but it was better to close them to minimize visual overload.

I gazed at Kazune in the capsule as she lay there with her eyes closed. Then, out of nowhere, her lips contorted, and her furrowed brow began to quiver as a single tear slipped out from between her lashes.

I'll never forget her last words. They were clear as day.

"It's just not fair... Why did *you* get to keep him...?"

• • •

That night, the three of us all slept in bed together for a change—me, Ryou, and our newly returned Kazune. Ryou was used to sleeping on his own like a big boy, so he complained at first, but he seemed a tiny bit happy about it. Or maybe I was just seeing what I wanted to see.

Once he fell asleep, Kazune and I talked in hushed tones.

"If 99 percent of the world's happiness is built on 1 percent of misery...what are we supposed to do? Do we still deserve it?" she asked me.

"...I don't know, but if we were given good lives, then I say we make the most of them. Otherwise, their misery will have been in vain... But then again, I suppose from their perspective, it *is* in vain."

"Yes, I suppose so..."

How did that 1 percent feel about the other 99 percent? Kazune 13's parting words were an indication.

"Still, I think we should lean in and embrace our happiness," I said. "And we should always seek out more. We're not *trampling* on that 1 percent—they're just a stepping stone for us."

"Don't you think it's wrong to use them like that?"

"There's no right or wrong about it. We're already standing here, on a mountain of possibilities. Our only option is to keep on living."

TO EVERY YOU I'VE LOVED BEFORE

"I suppose so."

Between us, Ryou lay snoring quietly. Kazune lovingly stroked his cheek, at which point I reached out and laid my hand on hers.

And before we went to bed, I vowed to her one more time: "I will love every you and all your possibilities...including the 1 percent this time."

In response, she answered, "I can see now just how blessed I truly am."

And I said, "Me too."

Interlude

TIME PASSED PEACEFULLY, all the way to our 60th birthdays.
One night, Ryou brought home a sweet, slightly timid girl named Eri-chan.

"Mom? Dad? We're thinking about marriage."

We had no reason to oppose the engagement. After all, it wasn't unexpected. We had met Eri-chan earlier, back when she and Ryou first started dating. Our only reaction was "Finally!" From there, we started bringing our families together in preparation for the wedding that was sure to follow sooner or later.

Then, two years later in the spring, Ryou finally said the magic words. It took longer than we were expecting, so we had quite a lot of money saved up for the ceremony. However, when we offered to throw them a lavish wedding, they told us they wanted something small and private. Boring, right?

Later that same night, however, there was a problem.

"Mom? Dad? We need some advice."

Eri-chan was spending the night that evening. She and Ryou came together to visit Kazune and I in our bedroom to talk about something. We both tensed up, dreading the worst. Whatever it was, the two of them couldn't seem to bring themselves to say it, and my mind was starting to take a dark turn.

"Well? What sort of advice did you need, son?" I asked, steeling myself. Kazune was listening intently too. They both looked so distraught, I could only imagine what grave horror was on their minds...

"Okay, here it is. We want to lock our IPs on the day of the wedding."

Oh. That's anti-climactic.

"It's just...when I think about what could happen if we shifted on the big day, it scares me... But if we lock our IPs, we'll be fine, right?"

As it turned out, Ryou and Eri-chan were experiencing the exact same fears *we* had felt prior to *our* wedding.

"You guys lock IPs at your work, right, Dad? So...could you maybe do it for us?"

Around this time, IP stabilization technology was becoming more widespread, and it was now legal for ordinary citizens to lock their IPs under special circumstances. Of course, they'd have to submit the proper forms and pass inspection, but at this point in our lives, Kazune and I had progressed further in our careers than we ever intended to. We had the authority to pull some strings here and there. So really, it was no wonder Ryou and Eri-chan had turned to us for help.

That said, if they were this hesitant to ask us about it, then they must have already realized that locking their IPs would mean eradicating all their other possibilities. Still, they wanted to marry their one and only beloved, and so they sought our input, regardless. In response, however, we neither supported nor rejected their wishes.

"Why don't we take a moment to reminisce about old times?" I suggested.

"Yes, that sounds nice," said Kazune.

And so we recounted our old memories, from our bizarre first encounter to her numerous rejections of me, from her half-assed confession of love to my half-assed proposal. Then we told them how we felt that same IP anxiety—though obviously we left out the story of our failed first night together. And then we told them about how we took our IP bands off for our wedding and married each other's possibilities. We told them about when Ryou was young—when we got caught up in a heinous crime, and I nearly broke my vow—and how happy we were now.

We relayed all of this to our dear, sweet children. It was really just a story we wanted to tell. However they chose to feel about it and whatever they decided as a result was up to them.

So, did they end up wearing their IP bands for their wedding, you ask?

Hmm, good question! You know, my memory's not as good as it used to be...

Yeah, let's go with that.

• • •

The next year, Ryou and Eri-chan had an adorable little girl who they named Ai. Sadly, both of my parents passed away before they got the chance to meet her. But with me, Kazune, Ryou, Eri-chan, and Ai, our family was large and happy enough already, so as new grandparents, we felt content to kick back and age like a fine wine.

Little Ai grew like a weed, and around the time she was in elementary school, my doctor discovered a tumor in my stomach. Luckily, they caught it at an early stage, so my treatment didn't take too harsh of a toll on my body. But Lady Luck was never on my side, and at the age of seventy-three, I was told I had six months to live. I figured I'd pass away in the hospital, but my family firmly insisted on another option.

When cancer patients approach the end of their life, they may choose to decline treatment or hospice care to instead spend their final days in the comfort of their own home. And when my son and his wife suggested I do the same, I felt truly blessed. I didn't want to be a burden on their family, but I trusted that they sincerely wanted to be there for me when my time came. It meant the world to me. And so, I agreed to stay at home under two conditions: no drugs, and no treatments.

At the age of seventy-three, I was perhaps still a bit too young to die, but oddly enough, I felt no fear or regret. I would finish out my life in a large house with my dear wife, my dependable son, my kindhearted daughter-in-law, and my adorable granddaughter. With my family at my side to see me off, even the most excruciating heart failure would be worth it to me. I had lived a good life.

Then I went home from the hospital and spent my remaining time with Kazune in peace...until that one day when my IP band announced my schedule.

At the end of each month, my device would list out all of the following month's scheduled events. At my age, I didn't do much socializing anymore, so I was puzzled as to what it was about to remind me of. That was when I learned of an appointment I had no recollection making.

August 17th, 10 a.m., Showa-dori intersection, Leotard Girl

To Every You
I've Loved Before

Epilogue...
or Prologue

JUST THEN, I snapped back to my senses.

In front of me was a crosswalk at a large intersection. The light was currently red, and cars were flying past. Now, what was I doing before I zoned out?

Ah, that's right. There was a girl standing on the crosswalk, and when I called out to her, she vanished. I thought maybe I parallel shifted, so I went to check my IP, only to find that my device was broken, and I was trying to figure out what to do about it.

I checked the IP band on my left wrist again.

ERROR

Definitely broken.

How odd—a moment ago, I felt uneasy at the prospect of not knowing my IP, but now, I wasn't scared at all. Actually, the more I thought about it, it didn't seem that odd at all.

When I was a kid, we didn't *have* IPs. Parallel worlds were the stuff of fiction, and people lived their lives blissfully unaware of them. Really, I just gone back to the way life used to be. Likewise, this world was a single die—I just couldn't see what side was facing up. Sure, this old dog was on his last legs, but that was no excuse to stop loving every world and their possibilities! The girl who vanished was still on my mind, but there was nothing I could do about it. I decided I would tell myself I merely saw a ghost.

Now then, I was in something of a pickle. I was *supposed* to be meeting someone here. Even though the IP function was glitched, the rest of my device still worked fine. Current time read 10:05. It was well past our meetup time, but I didn't see any familiar faces.

August 17th, 10 a.m., Showa-dori intersection, Leotard Girl.

I was definitely in the right place at the right time, so what was going on?

Granted, I didn't have any other plans today, so I could just wait and see. But unfortunately, this wasn't a park—it was a public intersection. If an old man in a wheelchair sat around here for too long, some good Samaritan might call the cops to take me home.

Still, seeing as I was already here, I could afford to wait, say, thirty minutes. With that thought, I rolled my wheelchair up onto the greenery by the statue where I wouldn't be in anyone's way. Then I turned myself to face the intersection—

"Hggh...!"

A familiar pain erupted in the pit of my stomach, like someone had wedged a wooden pestle into my chest and was crushing my innards. This pain struck at random intervals and triggered intense nausea every time. Sweating and breathing heavily, I pulled my pill case out of my pocket.

"Agh…!"

My hand was shaking so hard, I went and dropped the damn thing. I tried to lean over and grab it off the ground, but I couldn't possibly reach from in my chair. That said, if I got *out* of my wheelchair, there was no way I could get back into it on my own. Meanwhile, the pain was growing more and more intense with each passing moment, making it hard to think.

Boy, I hope I don't die here—would that be too much to ask? I'd rather take my last breath with Ai, Eri-chan, Ryou, and Kazune all there to see me off…

"…lo? Hello? Are you okay, dear?!"

Just then, I heard a woman's voice approaching. She sounded to be around my age. Whoever she was, she must have seen me struggling and come to my aid.

"I'll call you an ambulance—"

"My…pills…!" I groaned out.

"Huh?"

"Please…get my…pills…!"

Desperately, I pointed at the pill case lying at my feet. She saw it and immediately knelt down to grab it, unconcerned that her expensive-looking clothes would get dirty. That was how I knew she had to be a good person at heart.

"Now, which pills do you need?! There are a lot in here!"

"All of them… One of each…"

"Okay, one of each… This one, this one, this one… Here you are. Need a drink?"

I held out my hand, but she ignored it and brought the pills up to my lips with her own palm. She followed it up with a sip from her water bottle to wash them down.

"Should I still call you an ambulance?" she asked.

"No...I'm all right. Thank you, though..."

Over the next few minutes, my breathing slowed. Mind you, the medicine couldn't possibly work that fast; it was more will-power. A few minutes after that, I finally started to feel better. And when I slowly opened my eyes...I could scarcely believe it. The kindly woman was still standing there, watching over me with concern.

"Well now... It seems I really owe you one," I said to her.

"No, it's fine! Are you sure you're okay now?"

"Quite sure, thanks to you."

"Good! I'm so glad to hear it!" Her bright smile was the sweetest thing.

"You truly saved my life... I'd like to thank you somehow. Could I perhaps ask your name?"

"Oh, I'm no one special! I just did what anyone would do."

"But..." When I tried to protest, however, she broke out into a giggle. "What is it?" I asked.

"I just... Hee hee! I was hoping I'd get to drop that line before I died. 'I'm no one special!' Glad I made it right before the finish line," she said with a laugh.

"Ha ha! Well then, perhaps my blunder was worth it in the end."

"Oh, you!"

Though we'd never met before, the two of us laughed together like old friends. Then Kazune came to mind. Surely this didn't count as cheating, though, did it? Still...

"Say... Is it possible we've met somewhere before?" I asked.

"What?"

Wait—why in the world would I ask her such a thing?

She paused to scrutinize my face for a moment. "What's your name, sir?"

"Takasaki Koyomi."

"...Sorry, I don't think it sounds familiar."

I had her give me her name too, just in case, but sure enough, I didn't recognize it. Perhaps it was all in my head...or...

"Ah, I know. Perhaps we met in some parallel world somewhere," I mused.

"Ooh, that *is* a distinct possibility."

"And given our age, we might simply be too senile to remember it!"

"You're too funny! Hee hee hee!" she said, giggling again.

We shared another chuckle. For some reason, it was a blissful moment, and I was curious to know how this elegant old woman was feeling. "Have you lived a happy life?" I asked her.

Despite the sudden question, she didn't bat a lash. "Yes, I'm very happy," she replied, grinning from ear to ear.

"Glad to hear it!" Indeed, I truly was, from the bottom of my heart. "Now, how are you doing on time?"

"What?"

"Weren't you on your way somewhere?" I asked.

"No, no... Hee hee hee! Not at all, really. I was just out on a walk, and I felt like coming here today."

"Oh, I see."

"But you know, now that I've met you and had a little chat, I'm feeling very satisfied with my outing. I think I might walk right back home!" she said cheerfully.

"Well then, I'm sorry for keeping you."

"Don't be! I had a wonderful time. What about you?"

"Oh, I'm...waiting to meet with someone, you see," I said.

"Is that so! Well, I'd best run along."

"Right. Thanks again for all your help."

And so, having spread her cheer to me, the cheerful old woman briskly strolled over to the crosswalk and crossed the street.

I checked the time again. 11:00. For some reason I couldn't explain, I somehow *knew* that whoever I was waiting for wasn't coming.

No, the one *I* was waiting for wasn't here at this crosswalk at all.

"...Time to head back."

Back to Ai, back to Eri-chan, back to Ryou, and most of all, back to Kazune.

I left the empty intersection and went back to a world full of people I loved.

• • •

"Honey, I'm home."

"Welcome back." Kazune smiled softly at me as she watered her flowers in the yard. "How are you feeling?"

"Not bad, not bad." *Got a little dicey back there,* I thought to myself, but I decided not to mention it.

"So, did you solve the mystery?"

"No, sadly. No one showed up! I really don't know what that was about." It seemed I would never find out who I made those plans with…but oddly enough, part of me didn't mind too much.

"Koyomi, did something put you in a good mood?" she asked.

Now this came as a surprise. As far as I knew, I was acting like my usual self. Nevertheless, Kazune saw right through me.

"Well…instead of whoever I was waiting for, I had the most lovely encounter."

"Oh? Do tell."

As I recounted the story, I felt myself smile. "I met the happiest little old lady at the intersection."

"Lady?" Her expression turned threatening.

"Now, now, I'm too old to cheat. It wasn't like that."

"I'm just messing with you. Was it an old friend?"

"Total stranger, actually," I admitted.

"Really? What was so *lovely*, then?"

"Well, I'm glad to tell you about it if you'll listen."

"Yes, yes, I'm all ears," she replied, turning away to water the other flowers.

"She told me she was very happy with her life, and it really meant a lot to me."

"I thought you said she was a stranger."

"Yes. That's just it, Kazune."

"What?" She stopped and turned to look at me, and despite all the wrinkles, the surprise in her eyes was still adorable to behold.

"I didn't know her, but I was still so happy to hear that her life was going well." And I sincerely meant it from the bottom of my heart. "Isn't that just the loveliest thing? I'm so glad I grew up to be the sort of person who can celebrate a stranger's joy!"

Before I knew it, Kazune had set down her watering can and walked over to me. She put a wizened old hand on mine and listened warmly as I continued.

"I owe it to all the people in my life that I turned out this way. My father, my mother, my grandfather, my grandmother...Ryou, Eri-chan, Ai...and most of all..." I grasped her hand in kind and gazed into her eyes. "To you, Kazune. I wish I could send a message to every you I've loved before. I'd tell them how happy I am now—all because you were there."

"...I see." And with that, she gave me the sweetest smile I'd ever seen from her.

"Hey, Grandpa! Welcome hooome!"

Just then, I heard Ai shouting from inside the house. The phrase "indoor voice" simply wasn't in that girl's vocabulary.

"Hee hee... Shall we head in?"

"Yes, let's."

With her hand at my back, I went back inside my beloved home—the very portrait of happiness itself.

• • •

But before I go, there's someone else I'd like to send my message to.

To the countless other sides of my die, far more than just six—hundreds, thousands, millions! To every me in every distant world. To each and every me who loved someone other than Kazune.

Because *you* loved someone else, *I* loved Kazune. Thank you from the bottom of my heart. I've lived a truly blessed life.

And to that special someone other than Kazune, who loved a different me...

I send you all my gratitude and wish you the very best.

May you and your beloved find happiness somewhere in this world.

To Every You
I've Loved Before

The story *expands* in the breakthrough companion novel, out now from Seven Seas!

To Me, The One Who Loved You

by Yomoji Otono

In *Hidaka Koyomi's* world, travel between slightly different alternate universes is commonplace. After his parents' divorce, Hidaka now lives with his father. One day, he falls in love with a girl named *Satou Shiori* after meeting her at his father's workplace. Unfortunately, their young love seems doomed as their parents are getting remarried...to each other. Is there some parallel world out there where these two can be together as lovers, not step-siblings... and what could be the price if they try to find out?